THE ORDER OF DEATH

Former police detective Joseph Chrimes was happy in his retirement, relaxing with his plants and his cat, a peaceful existence that was shattered by a run of accidental deaths. 'Coincidence' said the police superintendent. 'Rubbish' retorted Chrimes who could not resist the challenge of investigating the deaths and searching for the common link. All of the victims had once played for the Grammar School cricket team, but surely somebody wasn't taking revenge for a beating many years earlier. When Chrimes does discover the link, he finds something astonishing in the order in which they are being eliminated...

THE ORDER OF DEATH

THE ORDER OF DEATH

by

Brian Bearshaw

Dales Large Print Books
Long Preston, North Yorkshire,
BD23 4ND, England.

British Library Cataloguing in Publication Data.

Bearshaw, Brian
  The order of death.

A catalogue record of this book is
available from the British Library

ISBN 1-84262-473-3 pbk
ISBN 978-1-84262-473-9 pbk

First published in Great Britain in 1979 by Robert Hale Ltd.

Published in Large Print 2006 by arrangement with
Robert Hale Limited

Dales Large Print is an imprint of Library Magna Books Ltd.

Printed and bound in Great Britain by
T.J. (International) Ltd., Cornwall, PL28 8RW

To Paul, Mark and Ruth

ONE

The naked, lifeless body floated smoothly down the river towards the weir that had once served Nuttleworth Mill. The soft glow of the moon, shining through the branches of the trees that lined the water, occasionally picked out the body as it flowed calmly on, face down. The left foot caught a large stone protruding a few inches out of the water, and the body swung round ever so gently like a roundabout just before it stops. It was just after two o'clock on a crisp, early-autumn Sunday morning, when the body drifted into the weir. The river was low and the body stuck on the huge stones that spanned the sixty feet of water, hardly moving as the river wandered peacefully by.

More than seven hours later, Andy, Ripper, and Hughie raced through the bluebell wood that took them to the river's edge. Andy and Ripper were the cowboys trying desperately to get to the fort before being killed by an arrow and scalped by the Injuns.

Hughie, that is.

'Keep 'em rollin',' screeched Andy, breathlessly, as they darted along the bank of the river. 'Almost there, pardner.'

The Injun put on speed and was within five yards of Ripper when he let out a blood-curdling scream that echoed through the valley.

'He's got me,' gasped Ripper, collapsing to his knees and clutching his chest.

Andy turned round in disgust. 'You're chicken,' he declared. 'Every time they get anywhere near you, you give in. It's a good job all cowboys weren't like you, or there wouldn't be any America. I'm not playing this any more,' he said, lifting his head towards Hughie.

Hughie wasn't listening. He was standing as if encased in cement, staring at the river, his eyes ready to pop out, unable to say a word, but one arm pointing. Andy and Ripper followed the direction of his arm to the centre of the weir where the body of Jeremy Moonsong, still naked, still lifeless, had come to rest.

'What is it?' enquired Ripper.

'It's a body, you fool,' snapped Andy.

Ripper's eyes opened wide, like Hughie's. 'Is it dead?'

'Course it is,' said Andy. 'Don't you know nothing?'

'How can you tell?'

'It isn't moving, is it?'

'Hughie isn't moving, but he isn't dead. Is he?'

'Anyway, people can't live in water,' declared Andy, knowledgably. 'They drown.'

At this moment, Hughie managed to speak. 'A body,' he croaked. 'Look, a body!'

'And it's dead,' stated Ripper, expounding his newly-acquired piece of information. 'Anyway, Andy says so.'

'What are we going to do?' said Hughie in a husky voice.

'I'm going to have a look at it,' said Andy firmly. He sat on the river bank, removed his boots and socks, and rolled up his trousers. Hughie and Ripper did the same and followed as Andy carefully edged his way along the stones to the body.

'It hasn't any clothes on,' said Ripper in a shocked tone as they got nearer. 'Looks like our baby,' he giggled.

'Shut up,' growled Andy.

'It can't hear, can it?' said Ripper, who was getting quite excited. 'What's it doing here anyway?'

As the three boys bent to have a closer

look at the back of the head of Jeremy Moonsong, a second body appeared round the bend of the river. It, too, was bare and dead, and was following exactly the same route as its predecessor.

The first the boys knew of the second arrival was when it gently bumped into the first. As it slowly turned to find its own resting place on the stones alongside the other body, Hughie let out an even more piercing, deafening shriek. Ripper started back in alarm, slipped on the slimy stone and sat with a bump in the river.

'What did you do that for?' he squealed.

'Here, I'm off,' croaked Andy, his eyes casting wildly up and down the river.

'Don't push,' Hughie managed to grunt. 'I'm going.'

Ripper managed to drag himself up and follow the other two to the bank. He was soaked to the waist and his trousers clung to his legs as he scampered along the stones to the river edge.

'I'm going for the police,' shouted Andy, setting off at the gallop through the wood. 'You two stay there.'

Hughie, his eyes agape, started to shake. 'Not me. I'm not staying here. Not with them two. You look after them,' he yelled at

Ripper as he raced after the fast-disappearing Andy.

Ripper turned for another look at the bodies, bare and gently bobbing. If he hadn't been on his own, he might have laughed. But he *was* on his own and it wasn't funny. 'Hey, wait for me,' he called as he seized his shoes and socks and hurtled after his friends.

By the time the police arrived twenty-five minutes later, the third body had arrived. It rested five yards from its companions, facing them, but not acknowledging them. All the faces were in the dirty chemical-ridden water, and there was little to distinguish one from another.

TWO

The coroner, Mr Sidney Bull, laid his glasses on the desk, leaned forward, and said: 'There can be no doubt, can there, Dr Armstrong, that all three died from drowning.'

'No doubt at all,' replied Dr Armstrong, consultant pathologist, who had conducted post mortems on the three bodies.

'And the only mark on any of them was a small bump on the temple on Mr Moonsong?'

'That's right. On the hairline above the right eye.'

'Could you say, Dr Armstrong, whether such a blow would be sufficient to render the deceased unconscious?'

'That's difficult to say. I would say probably not, but it is impossible to be definite.'

'Is it possible to say what caused the wound? Could it have happened accidentally if he had dived into the river?'

'Yes, that is quite possible.'

'And, of course, somebody could have struck him on the head. It's fair to say that?'

'Yes indeed.'

The inquest on Jeremy Moonsong, Richard Hazelton, and Thomas Pike was held in the No 1 Courtroom at the Magistrates Court at Skelham. Sidney Bull, a partner in a firm of family solicitors who had operated in the town for more than a hundred years, had grown enormously in self importance when he was appointed Borough Coroner, and he revelled in the opportunity to occupy the magistrates bench in the No 1 Courtroom whenever he had the opportunity.

The curious deaths of the three men had caused a stir in the large, northern market town where all were prominent citizens and reasonably well-known.

Jeremy Moonsong, 43 years old, married with two teenage children, had been an accountant in the town since leaving school. Richard Hazelton, aged 37 and a bachelor, ran a flourishing grocery business on the market square, and Tom Pike, 48, married with one grown-up son, was assistant manager of the Midland Bank. The first two had both attended Skelham Grammar School and were members of the town cricket club. Pike was a relative newcomer to the town, having arrived 14 years earlier from the Midlands. And it was he, so the town gossip had it, who had led on the other two to the stupid challenge that had resulted in the tragic death of all three.

The two widows were at the inquest, close together in a corner of the public seats at the back of the courtroom, which was unusually crowded on this sunny afternoon.

It transpired that the three men had been in the habit of going to the Archduke Ferdinand, a popular pub on the edge of town overlooking the River Lang, every Saturday night. Evidence was given by the licensee, Reg Perkins, who said he had overheard the three of them arguing their merits as swimmers.

'They were like big lads,' he told the coroner. 'One of them, Mr Pike, I believe it was, boasted about how he had been school champion and reckoned he could still give anybody a race over a short distance. He was always boasting was Mr Pike, reckoned he had done the 100 metres freestyle in under a minute when he was at school. They tell me the world record isn't much faster than that,' he added.

'Anyway, one thing led to another, and at the finishing up, Mr Pike bangs a ten-pound note on the bar top and tells the others to match that if they think they can beat him over 50 metres. It was nearly closing time and I had to get on with my work – there were a lot of customers – so I never saw whether the two gentlemen decided to take him on. In any case, I'd have thought they'd have gone to the baths to settle their wager, not to the river at that time of night.'

The licensee of the Archduke Ferdinand said all the men had been in the public house, he thought, for at least three hours, maybe longer ... 'and they'd supped quite a bit, I can tell you.'

Dr Armstrong was able to be more specific about the amounts the men had drunk. All were beer drinkers and the pathologist estimated Hazelton and Pike's consumption at about nine pints each, but Moonsong's considerably less – no more than four.

Detective Chief Inspector Harry Rackham, who had conducted the investigation into the tragedy, said he had failed to find anybody who had witnessed the bizarre Saturday night bathe in the River Lang.

'Nobody else went along from the public house, and there seems little doubt that these three men struck their bet and went immediately to the river to settle it,' he said. 'They went to a spot about half a mile away – they were all in Mr Moonsong's car –

where the river narrows and is about five feet deep. There's a long straight stretch there, about 120 yards I should say, and...'

'Would you mind expressing that in metres, Chief Inspector?' interrupted the coroner, loftily.

'Beg pardon, sir,' said the detective. 'About 110 metres. The car was parked nearby, the men undressed there, and entered the water at this point.'

'The clothes were all there, were they, with the car?' the coroner enquired.

'Not quite, sir. Mr Hazelton and Mr Pike's clothes were in the car, but Mr Moonsong, it seems, had decided to undress outside. His clothes were on the river bank.'

'I see. But at the same spot?'

'Yes sir.'

'Very good, Chief Inspector. So these men get into the water, naked, ready to swim some distance – we don't know how far – in a foolhardy attempt to settle some wager. That seems clear. But is there any evidence at all to show how they came to meet their tragic deaths?'

'No sir. None at all. It does seem that Mr Moonsong could have lost consciousness by striking his head on a stone.'

'Assuming he dived in?'

'Yes sir. After that it is difficult to tell what happened. The two other men had had quite a good deal to drink and it is possible that, realising Mr Moonsong's plight, they attempted to rescue him. The water flows reasonably fast at this point and as the body was being carried away, they could have given chase. It was a clear, moonlit night, but the banks of the river are heavily wooded, and it was light only in patches. What with the drink, the plight of Mr Moonsong, and the darkness, it is possible that the two men floundered about in the water before being overcome, probably by fatigue, and were drowned.'

'It all seems very odd, Chief Inspector. Was there any evidence of foul play?'

'None at all, sir. All the men were respected and esteemed in the town and despite exhaustive enquiries I have not been able to discover any reason why anybody should want any of them dead. And certainly, there was nothing at the car or the surrounding area to suggest foul play. And as Dr Armstrong said, apart from the lump on Mr Moonsong's forehead, which could have been caused by him diving in, there were no marks on the bodies.'

'In your view then, Chief Inspector...?'

'In my opinion, sir, and on the evidence we have, it seems that these men were the victims of a stupid prank. It was a childish thing to do, the sort of antic rugby players get up to, if you understand my meaning, sir.'

'As president of Skelham Rugby Football Club, I don't understand your meaning at all, Chief Inspector,' boomed the coroner in a pompous tone. 'All you mean to say is that perhaps the drink had got the better of their good sense and they decided to settle their wager there and then?'

'Quite so sir,' replied the detective, sheepishly.

'Another point,' said the coroner. 'Why were these men not missed until their bodies were found? None of them had been home. Didn't their wives wonder where they were?'

'As you know sir, Mr Hazelton was a bachelor. He lived alone, so there wasn't anybody to miss him. And it seems in any case that these gentlemen had, in the past, stayed the night at his flat, playing cards. It wasn't unusual, so their wives didn't wait up for them.'

After listening to the evidence for an hour and a half, the coroner returned an Open verdict.

'This has been an extremely unusual, one might almost say, unique, story,' he declared. 'I certainly cannot recall having heard anything like it in my 15 years experience as Her Majesty's Coroner to this Borough. There seems little doubt that these men did travel to the river intending to settle their argument. That is clear from the evidence. They removed their clothes, but whatever happened after that we just cannot tell. The most likely explanation is that Mr Moonsong unfortunately banged his head in diving into the water and that his companions sacrificed their lives in their attempts to save him. But there are too many unknown factors for me to record a definite verdict.'

THREE

'That's queer.' Donald Margerison rested the Skelham Evening Argus on his knees, and from the depths of his armchair by the fire, he looked across the room to his wife. He had not asked a question, but the remark demanded a response, and his wife, Roseanne, put down the plates she had collected from the table, returned her husband's earnest stare, and dutifully asked: 'What's queer, dear?'

Donald took off his slipper and scratched the sole of his foot. 'Ray McCarthy's dead,' he declared. 'He's the fifth Old Boy from the school to have died in the last few weeks. Not only that, four of them were about my time.'

'Fancy that. Wasn't one of those fools who drowned in the river a couple of weeks ago, wasn't he at school with you?'

'That's right. Poor old Jeremy Moonsong. One of the others, Richard Hazelton, was at school as well, but he was a bit after us. And if you remember, about two weeks before that, George Heritage fell while climbing in the Lakes and was killed. And who was the other one who died? Who was that now?'

Donald was out of his chair now, his brow furrowed as he stood with his back to the fire and felt the warmth seep through his trousers. 'That's it,' he exclaimed, turning excitedly to his wife. 'Ian Boyd, killed when his aeroplane crashed taking off at Roches Clear. Dear old Ian. Dickie we called him, you know, my dear,' he said with a smile.

'Yes, you told me,' she said in a bored tone that suggested she had heard why a dozen times before, but knew there was no way of avoiding being told again.

'That's right. Dickie Boyd. You get it? Dickie ... Boyd.'

'Yes dear. It's hit your cricket team as well, hasn't it? You're going to be a player or two short, aren't you?'

The fond memory of Dickie Boyd that had brought the flicker of a smile to Donald's lips quickly faded as he took in the full meaning of his wife's remark.

'Isn't that strange?' he said. 'I hadn't really thought about that. You're right. Dickie and Jeremy gone. Opening bat and our best seamer. Wow! That's a sock in the eye for the club, two great stalwarts like them having gone. And Ray McCarthy used to turn out for us on occasions when we were stuck. I say ... bit of a blow, what?'

'Well, I don't know about your opening bat, but any seaming you want doing, Gladys Parker's very good, you know.'

'Gladys Parker,' repeated Donald, incredulously. 'Gladys Parker! What does she know about cricket? From what I know of Gladys Parker she doesn't know a square leg from a wooden leg.'

'You wanted a seamer, didn't you? Well, Gladys is a wonder with a sewing machine. Any seaming you want, anything taking in or letting out, Gladys is first rate.'

Donald stared in disbelief. 'All the years I've been playing cricket,' he exclaimed. 'And you've learnt nothing. Nothing! A seamer has nothing to do with a sewing machine. He's a seam bowler, a special sort of bowler who uses the seam on the ball to make it break away at different angles.'

'Oh well, I don't know,' said Roseanne, resuming her collection of the pottery from tea. 'It's like a foreign language to me.'

Roseanne hurriedly gathered together the plates, cups and saucers, pudding dishes and cutlery into one dangerously insecure pile, and then skilfully carried them through

25

to the kitchen. Donald watched her, waiting, as he did every night, for the crash that never came, and then steered his thoughts back to school, and the Old Boys who had just lost their lives.

Unaccountably, a cold shudder ran up Donald's spine. He sat quietly and thought carefully. Four men, they had all been at school at the same time as himself, all killed in unusual circumstances. All... Heavens! Ray McCarthy only played cricket from time to time now, but he, too, had been in the school team! It was uncanny. It wouldn't have been so bad if one of them had died in his bed from something fairly normal like cancer. But no. An aeroplane crash, a climbing accident, Jeremy drowned, and Ray ... the victim of a hit-and-run driver. That was stretching coincidence a bit far, wasn't it? All violent deaths. And ... Donald shivered again ... all either played cricket or had played the game. The more he thought about it, the more incredible it all seemed. He would have thought there was some jinx on the school cricket team, but George Heritage had only just made the second team. Hadn't even got his second eleven colours as far as he could remember.

Even so, this precise falling together of so

many facts really was remarkable. He wondered if anybody else had noticed the connection.

'Roseanne! Roseanne!'

The kitchen door opened, and Roseanne, a tea towel in one hand and a plate in the other, stood at the entrance.

'This is deucedly odd,' declared Donald. 'I've been thinking about these four who were killed.'

'I thought you said five.'

'Discount Hazelton for the moment. He was younger than the rest of us. A lot younger. But the other four were all at school at the same time as me, we all played cricket, they've all died in very strange circumstances.'

Roseanne closed the door and leaned against it.

'What are you saying?' she asked quietly. 'Are you suggesting, perhaps, that somebody is responsible for all their deaths. One person has killed them all and made them look like accidents. And it all has something to do with cricket. That sounds even more unbelievable.'

'I think I might have a word with Matt Thornton, the club president,' said Donald. 'He's a superintendent in the police and he's an Old Boy of the school. A sight older than me, too, I can tell you. Though I do remember playing against him a couple of times when the school played the Old Boys. I can talk to him. I daresay he'll put my mind at rest.'

'You could call tomorrow, at lunch time. But don't be surprised, Donald, if they laugh you out of the building.'

Superintendent Matt Thornton did laugh, the typical booming laugh of a fat man, his several chins wobbling as he rocked in his chair.

'Now come on Donald, old boy,' he gulped. 'You're not seriously suggesting some bod is trying to knock off a cricket team. Or he's got some grudge against Skelham Royal Grammar School. What? Eh?'

Donald knew it could all be made to sound stupid. He couldn't really see any sense in it himself.

'But surely, Mr President, you've got to admit it's all very odd,' he declared intently. 'All these Old Boys of the school, all...'

'Yes, yes, yes, I know what you're saying,' the superintendent interrupted testily. 'All from the same school at the same time, and all cricketers. What motive would anybody have for murdering a cricket team, or a group of people like this. Tell me that, eh?'

'I don't know. I thought if you investigated, if the police at least had a look at it, it might throw up some reason. There could be some link between all these people that we don't know anything about.'

'Now look here, Donald. Harry Rackham, who looked into the deaths of those three in the river, is a first-class officer. No reason why he shouldn't rise even higher in the Force. A man with many of the attributes needed to become a superintendent. Thorough, sensible, persistent, he gets into a case. Now I know he left no stone unturned in this case, and there was not a scrap of evidence, not a scrap, to suggest that these men had been anything other than the victims of a stupid, childish prank.'

'Yes, but...'

'No buts. No evidence. No suggestion whatsoever of foul play. He even matched up the footprints at the spot where the car had been left, and other than the three men's, there was none. He combed the area, too, in search of the instrument with which an assailant might have struck poor old Moonsong. Nothing. He enquired into their backgrounds, their private and business lives, and there wasn't a shred...' he shook his head vigorously as he said this, and his chins slapped back and forth indecently .... 'not a shred of scandal or dishonour touched their names. There was no reason at all for the deaths of these men. In any case, one of them didn't even attend the school, did he, and the other was some years after this time you're speaking about. No, Donald, no. There's no sense to it.'

Donald looked at the carpet and the foot of the superintendent's desk. He could pick out a line of dust near the bottom. He itched to get a duster to it.

'I know this, Mr President,' he said, resignedly. 'It just seems too many coincidences all together.'

'These things do happen, Donald, old boy. Pity about Boyd. Good player, good player. You were in the team with him at school, weren't you? I seem to recall being in the Old Boys team when we played the school one year when you two were in the side. Am I right, eh, or am I wrong?'

'You're quite right, Mr President. That's what I was saying, of course. Jeremy Moonsong, Dickie Boyd, Ray McCarthy and George Heritage, all at school at the same time as me, all played cricket. Although

George wasn't quite so good as the others. Didn't make the first team. In fact, if I remember right, he only had one season in the second team. Not a particularly good player. Ray McCarthy I never really understood. He was a good batsman, but once he left school he never seemed really interested in the game. He came to the club for a year or two, but then gave it up seriously, just playing the occasional game when he felt like it.'

The superintendent reached in his jacket pocket for his pipe. 'He was married young, wasn't he? Makes a difference you know, Donald. How's the wife, by the way? Angela, isn't it?'

'Roseanne actually, Mr President.'

The police officer banged the desk with the flat of his hand. 'That's right. Roseanne. Of course it is. Knew there was an Ann in there somewhere. And the children, they're all right?'

'Just the one, Mr President. Jennifer. She's fine.'

'Good, good. These deaths have taken something out of the community, of course, Donald. You don't need me to tell you that. Young men, virtually, all of them. Got on, many of them, as well. What's your job now, Donald?'

31

'Still with the Building Society, Mr President. Joined them from school. Joint deputy assistant manager now.'

'Is that so? Well, well. You'd know these men pretty well, wouldn't you? Very upsetting. Like I say, a piece cut out of the community, and boys I have known myself. George Heritage ... killed climbing, wasn't he?'

'That's right. Went to the Lakes for the weekend on his own. Used to go up quite often, I understand, and usually on his own. Preferred it that way. He took the usual precautions. Told the guest house where he was staying, which peak he was going to, and when he hadn't arrived by the middle of the evening, a rescue team was sent out. He hadn't fallen far, apparently, only about thirty feet, but he had fractured his skull and was dead when they got to him. Have they found anybody for McCarthy's death yet? Hit and run, wasn't it?'

'Yes, out on the Grane Road. Near where he lived, it seems. In the habit of going to the local for a drink most nights and being so near he'd walk it. There's no path there and he was on his way back when this Mad Harry hit him. Nobody saw it, but from the distance he was thrown I'd say the car must have been shifting. We've got an alert out for the car. It must have a dent on it, and it could be pretty big, and there was red paint on McCarthy's clothes. Gives us a good chance of catching the blighter. And soon, too. Well, it has been good to see you, Donald. Do call in again, any time. And my regards to your good lady. Mandy, isn't it?'

'Thank you for you time, Mr President,' said Donald as he rose from his chair. He had just reached the door when the superintendent called him.

'By the by, Donald. That boy you said didn't play cricket very much. Heritage, the one killed climbing. You were wrong, you know. He did play for the school team once that I know of – in the end-of-season match with the Old Boys. I know. I played for the Old Boys and clean bowled him first ball. I'm surprised you forgot that.'

FOUR

George Heritage had played for the school first team! That made the whole thing even more incredible. The links between the four dead men were stronger than ever now, and whatever doubts the superintendent had build in Donald's mind while he was in the police station, they had certainly disappeared with that last bit of information.

It was in the middle of a particularly dull and pointless play on television that evening that Donald decided on his next course of action.

'Roseanne!' Donald always started a conversation with his wife by first making sure she was awake and attentive. He would not start until she acknowledged his call to order.

'Roseanne!'

His wife was dozing. She didn't really mind dull, pointless plays from time to time. They could be beautifully soporific after a good meal and she enjoyed a quiet nap in front of the fire. She had heard Donald's first call, but had kept quiet in the hope that he might realise she was half asleep and decide to not pursue whatever it was he wanted to transmit. She ignored the second call in the hope that he might, just for once, carry on talking without waiting for her to reply.

'ROSEANNE, I'm talking to you!'

The third call positively demanded attention and Roseanne knew it was no good continuing to disregard her husband. She stretched herself slowly, yawned loudly and pointedly, and said: 'Did you call dear?'

'I've been thinking. I told you Matt Thornton wouldn't have anything to do with me. Thought the suggestion that the deaths are linked was ridiculous, then went and tied them together even more strongly.'

'Laughed at the idea, didn't he dear?'

'You know, I just can't understand the police, Roseanne. I suppose they must get so obsessed with cars on yellow lines, political demonstrations and picket lines, that they can't see wholesale murder when it's right under their noses these days.'

'Yes dear,' obliged Roseanne.

'Well, I'm not forgetting about it. The whole thing's far too fishy to dismiss without some sort of investigation.'

'Where else can you go, dear?'

'You remember that other policeman we used to know long ago, when Jennifer was a toddler. He used to come up to the cricket club in those days, he'd been at the school and was quite a lively old stick. Rose to be an inspector, I think. Maybe even chief inspector. He used to bounce about the place, full of life, and a thundering voice that used to sound for miles around.'

'Oh yes,' agreed Roseanne, showing genuine interest for the first time. 'He was a lovely man. Very tall and erect, I remember, always busy, never still. But he always had a word and a pocketful of sweets for the children to dip into. And couldn't he shout? There'd been some sort of a do at the club once and we needed the floor clearing and the dishes washing. He just stood in the centre of the floor and bellowed like a sergeant-major. I've never seen people move so quickly.'

'What was his name? Something queer.'

'Chrimes, wasn't it?'

'That's right. Joseph Chrimes. And he insisted on the Joseph, too. Never had Joe. Thought Joseph a strong, lovely old name.'

'It is, too. And you're going to see him? See if he will take you any more seriously than the superintendent did. But didn't he retire some years ago?'

'That's right. He did. Not all that long ago, I don't think. I'll have to find out where he lives and I'll go along there.'

'Didn't he live in one of those nice houses up near Auntie Mary's. You know, that quiet little cul-de-sac round the corner from St George's. Spring Close, that's it. Saw him going there once. Second house up on the right I think it was. When are you going to go?'

'Right away,' replied Donald. 'Tomorrow afternoon.'

The following day was a Saturday and with his plan of campaign formed, Donald was able to concentrate on his work in the morning. After a quick meal at home he set off to walk the mile and a half to Spring Close, leaving his car in the garage and deciding to give himself the extra time to organise his thoughts and present his argument thoroughly.

St George's Church stood on the outskirts of the town, a building erected in the early 1920s to meet the extra demands of a growing community. The houses in Spring Close had been built about the same time, substantial dwellings, roomy, well-planned, and built to last. The second house on the right was number 4 and Donald walked up the flagged path, which looked as if it had only recently been swept clean of leaves, to the white front door. He knocked, waited, then knocked again. He tried a third time and when there was no reply he set off back down the path. He was near the gate when he heard a shout from the house next door. It was an elderly woman with beautiful white hair.

'Have you tried round the back?' she called in a high-pitched voice. 'He's usually in there after dinner.' She pointed to the path running down the side of the house and Donald re-traced his steps and through a wicker gate.

As he rounded the corner of the house, he heard a faint, rhythmic sound, like sawing. His eyes quickly cast round the neat, well-tendered garden, but there was no sign of anybody. He listened carefully and then followed the sound which led him to a small extension to the house, a sun lounge where dozens of plants lined the shelves. The top half of the room was composed entirely of glass and Donald quickly established the cause of the noise.

In a comfortable-looking armchair at the

opposite end of the room sat Joseph Chrimes. His head was resting on his chin and he was fast asleep and snoring gently. On his lap lay a sleek, black cat, as soundly asleep as its master. It was a mild day with only the occasional lazy murmuring of a reluctant breeze, and apart from the spasmodic sound of a contented thrush, the only noise to disturb the silence, was the snoring of Joseph Chrimes.

Donald looked at him in dismay. This was not the exuberant man he remembered, bursting with life and oozing endeavour. He could have been ninety. He was wearing a striped, flannelled, collarless shirt, unbuttoned to reveal a scraggy neck. He must have removed his teeth, for his bottom lip was almost touching his nose. He was wearing blue braces and his old constable's trousers that were unfastened at the waist, revealing the top of his woollen underpants. He had slipped his heels out of his sheepskin slippers and his feet were resting on a small, soft pouffe. A half-drunk pot of tea was on a small table at his elbow and Donald could just make out the remains of a meat and potato pie on a plate which he had deposited on top of an empty plant pot.

Donald knew he had made a mistake. He

shouldn't have come. Mr Chrimes was retired now, and living the way all retired gentlemen should, in the peace and quiet of their own homes, with a black cat and a pot of tea for company. He turned to leave, but as he moved, his foot knocked over an empty milk bottle and sent it clattering along the path.

The noise startled the cat who let out an anguished cry as it jumped off its master's knee. Mr Chrimes came out of his stupor much more slowly, but just in time to see Donald, his shoulders hunched, tip-toeing away to the gate.

'Hey, who's that?' he called as he pushed himself into an upright position in the chair. 'Let's be seeing you!'

Donald turned, unwillingly. 'Just me, Mr Chrimes,' he called. 'You won't remember me, I'm from...'

'Oh yes, I do,' declared Mr Chrimes. 'Never forget a face, I don't. No, never. Get along in 'ere, the door's open, and I'll give you a name, that I will.'

There was no escape now, so Donald opened the door and went into the sun lounge. The room had soaked up the morning sun and the room was pleasantly and lethargically warm. Tomatoes had obviously been grown there during the summer for the tangy, distinctive smell was still lingering.

Mr Chrimes studied Donald for several seconds without saying a word. At close range he presented an even sorrier picture to Donald, who was hypnotised by a face that uncannily resembled a tired bassett hound. The eyes were heavy with sleep, the skin was sagging, and Donald thought there was nothing as undignified as a human being without teeth. The older man slowly and ruminatively stroked his chin which had not been shaved that day.

'Margerison!' he said finally in triumph. 'Donald Margerison!' He laughed and Donald got a nauseating glimpse of naked gums that made him wish again that he had seen that milk bottle and been able to avoid it when he turned.

'Cricket club, isn't it? You're after a vice-president, aren't you?'

'No, nothing like that, Mr Chrimes.' Donald laughed nervously, wondering how to escape.

Mr Chrimes seemed as fascinated with Donald's face as Donald was revolted by his. The older man continued to stare, and then nodded. ''Ow's that nice young wife of yours, Roseanne? A little beauty, that one, if I remember. Could 'ave fancied 'er myself, I could 'ave,' he continued, huskily.

'She's fine, just fine,' said Donald, nervously shifting his weight from one leg to the other.

''Ere, sit you down.' Mr Chrimes waved to a chair behind the door. 'Forgetting my manners I am. Old age, you see, Donald, you start to forget. Well, if it isn't a vice-president you want, and I don't suppose you're 'ere to sell that delightful good lady of yours, what can I be a doing of for you?'

He gripped the arms of his chair and with an effort, started to lever himself slowly to his feet. Donald sprang off the chair ready to assist. 'Can I help?'

Mr Chrimes dropped back into the chair with a grunt of relief. 'Pass me that mug will you, Donald, and the pipe next to it.' He pointed to a shelf behind Donald's chair.

Donald reached for the mug and almost dropped it when he saw the elderly man's false teeth rocking about in the water. Mr Chrimes took them out of the mug, gave them a quick shake, and then, with the adroitness of a master magician, popped them into immediate position in his mouth. As he stuffed the bowl of the pipe with tobacco from a pouch in his trousers pocket, he said again: 'Now then. What is it as I can be a doing of for you?'

Suddenly, the whole thing seemed non-sensical to Donald again. This man would be asleep before he was a quarter the way through, and in any case, what would it sound like to a man of his age, wrapped in tomatoes and Busy Lizzie plants.

'Oh, it's nothing really, honestly,' said Donald, hesitantly. 'Really.'

Mr Chrimes studied Donald as he set fire to his tobacco. A serious young man, he remembered. Not much fun about him, but a willing, capable young man. Dull, but pleasant, hard-working but ... so deadly serious.

'It must be quite a few years since we last saw one another,' the old man muttered. 'The wife was still living then, we used to get up to the cricket club just about every weekend. So I daresay it could be top side of ten years since I saw you. Now I can't believe, Donald, that you've come to see me, after all these years ... about nothing. So come on lad, cough it up. Might be a gold watch.'

There was nothing else for it. Donald would have to go through his unlikely theory, whether he wanted to or not. He would keep it short and then beat a hasty retreat while the old man was falling off his chair with hysterics.

'Did you see about that hit-and-run in the paper this week, Ray McCarthy killed, chief wages clerk at Butler's, an Old Boy of the school,' declared Donald after a deep breath.

'Can't say as 'ow I did,' Mr Chrimes replied. 'I gets the paper, but don't always 'as the right opportunity to go through it. Saw about them three lads as was drownded in the river, though. Funny do that.'

'And then there was old Dickie Boyd...'

'Aeroplane crashed, didn't it?'

'Yes, and George Heritage...'

'George 'Eritage, that rings a bell. Rotary isn't 'e?'

'Not now. He's dead as well.'

'Crimes! Is that right? Well, well, well, I'm blessed. All of 'em gone, 'as they? Is it some sort of a monument you're thinking of then?'

'No. No, it was just that it all seemed so queer. Such a coincidence.'

Mr Chrimes had hardly taken his eyes off Donald's face. The lad was obviously agitated about something and wanted his advice. But he wasn't presenting his case at all well.

'I don't understand, Donald,' he said gently and still in a husky voice. 'Where's the coincidence?'

'Well,' replied Donald, warming to the account once more, 'they were all at the school at the same time, all in the first eleven for cricket, and all died within a short time of one another in mysterious circumstances.'

'You were in the school team, weren't you, Donald? Captain one year if I remember when I was in the Old Boys team.'

'I didn't remember you playing, Mr Chrimes.'

'Oh yes, quite a few years I did. A decent bat, too, even if I does say so as shouldn't. Come to think of it, I've an idea as 'ow I came into conflict with all of those men on a cricket field. You were about the same time, wasn't you?'

The cat, which had been washing itself by an ornate mirror leaning against the wall in a corner of the room, decided it was peaceful enough to return to its master's lap. The old man stretched out his legs again, settled himself more comfortably in his chair, and rested his feet on the pouffe. Donald decided he would have to be quick, or the scene that had greeted his arrival would soon be back.

'That's right. We played together. I got into the side the year one or two of them were leaving. I didn't think George Heritage had played in the first team until I was reminded by...'

''Ow'd 'e die, 'Eritage?'

'He was killed climbing.'

Mr Chrimes puffed at his pipe, and didn't say anything for a few seconds. Then: 'I'm sorry, I interrupted. You was saying as 'ow somebody reminded you.'

'Yes, I couldn't remember him having got into the first team, but Matt Thornton, he...'

'The superintendent? You've been to see 'im? And what did Super Duper 'ave to say about it all?'

'He laughed at me,' said Donald. 'Nearly fell off his chair. Put it all down to coincidence.'

'But you don't? Why not?'

'It's stretching coincidence too far to expect four men, all about the same age, who all went to the same school, played in the school cricket team, to die at about the same time.'

'And not a one of 'em a natural death, as

you'd say.'

'No. An aeroplane crash, climbing accident, a hit-and-run, and a drowning.'

'Tell me something, Donald. If these weren't accidents, what would you say 'as been 'appening?'

'I don't know,' declared Donald, lifting his arms and looking towards the ceiling dramatically. 'I just don't know, but it's not right.'

'Well, if they're not accidents, somebody, somewhere, is responsible for the lot. That's what you're saying, Donald, isn't it? There's a murderer running wild. But why? What for? You must 'ave thought a lot about this, to go to the police and then me. You think per'aps 'e's got it in, this mysterious man, for a cricket team.'

'Sounds daft, doesn't it,' said Donald, disgustedly. 'It makes some sort of sense when it's running about in my head. But put it into words, start discussing it, and I start sounding like a raving lunatic. I'm sorry I disturbed you, Mr Chrimes. I'll not waste any more of your time.'

He got out of his seat, and turned to the door. He had only gone a stride when he was deafened by a bellow from the middle of the armchair.

'SIT DOWN!' The cat leapt in the air and

scuttled back to its corner. Donald fell back into his chair, and Mr Chrimes took another long, satisfying puff on his pipe.

'Matt Thornton. Now 'e 'as no imagination whatsoever. That's 'ow 'e got to be superintendent. Followed the line. It was 'Arry Rackham, if I remember, 'oo investigated them drownings. 'E's thorough, is 'Arry, sees a thing through, but 'e needs to believe in something to really get 'is teeth into it. I was the same, though 'as 'ow it's me that's saying it as shouldn't, but when 'Arry knows 'e's onto something, 'e's like a terrier with a rat. But if 'e don't believe with all 'is 'eart, 'e misses them little things that matter. Now, I can only assume that all these cases, dealt with separately – and two of them weren't in this area – satisfied the officer in charge as to their accidental nature. The 'it and run we'll 'ave to see about.'

Donald had recovered himself. The cat was still sulking near the mirror, but Donald was sitting on the edge of his chair. 'You think there could be something in it, then, Mr Chrimes?' he asked, excitedly.

'Well, I must admit it's as queer as any 'owdoyoudo 'as I've ever 'ad the good fortune to come across,' came the reply. 'Tell you what do, Donald.' He smiled.

'Yes,' said Donald, eagerly.

'You leave this 'ere with me. I know a few folk and I'll start asking a question or two. Circumspectly.' He pronounced each syllable of the last word slowly and quietly, and tapped his nose with his forefinger. 'I'll see what the word is. And I'll tell you something, Donald.'

Donald didn't say a word this time, but sat open-mouthed, hanging on every word that the former police officer said.

'If your 'unch is correct, crimes, this'll be the biggest slaughter in Skelham since the Plague. So we'll leave it at that then, Donald. And I'll be getting in touch.'

Donald left the way he had entered and turned in time to see Mr Chrimes replacing his teeth in the mug of water and settling himself down in his chair again.

'And don't forget, Donald!' he called. 'Cir-cum-spec-tion.'

FIVE

Two days later, just a few minutes after Donald had arrived home from work, there was a loud, insistent knocking at the front door. Donald had removed one shoe and hurried to finish putting on his slippers before answering the door. But before he could complete the operation there came an even more deafening hammering. With one slipper in his hand he scurried into the passageway just in time to see the letter box flip open.

'ANYBODY 'OME?' a voice bellowed through it. 'COME ON, COME ON, COME ON! Let's be 'aving you!'

Donald sped along the hall, turned the lock, and flung open the door to reveal a tall, upright man in a black bowler hat and a dark grey, well-cut overcoat with a black velvet collar. The street light shone in his shoes, over his arm was an umbrella, and in one hand a pair of black gloves.

'Y-e-e-s,' stammered Donald, disturbed for a moment by the noisy demands of his

51

visitor. 'What do you want?'

The man peered forward. ''As you forgotten me in two days then, Donald. Eh, 'as you?'

Donald looked more closely at the man's face. 'Good grief, it's you Mr Chrimes, isn't it? I didn't recognise you for the minute. Do come in. Please.' He stepped back, and his visitor, with long, purposeful steps, strode into the hall and straight into the living room at the end of the passage.

Donald was slow to recover from the shock. Was this well-groomed, eager individual the same doddering old man he had seen only two days before. The transformation was unbelievable. He hadn't even recognised him at first. He hurried to join his visitor.

Mr Chrimes was seated in front of the fire, his back straight, his hands resting on his umbrella which was between his feet.

'Grand 'ouses these, Donald,' he declared. 'There's substance to them. Craftsmen built these 'ouses and gave you plenty of room. Can't do with them modern boxes they keep putting up these days. Give me something substantial, Donald. Sub-stan-tial. Now then, down to business.'

Donald sat down, facing the former policeman.

'For the last two days I 'ave made enquiries into the deaths of the four gentlemen we mentioned. A bit of news first that you might not 'ave 'ad the good fortune to 'ear. About Mr McCarthy. The car which 'it 'im on 'is way back from the pub was found five miles away. It was identified easily enough, and turned out to belong to a man not unknown to me, or to you either I daresay, the former 'Ead of languages at Skelham Royal Grammar School and 'imself an Old Boy at the school, Mortimer Shelby.'

Mr Chrimes beamed at Donald from over the top of his umbrella. 'A most interesting piece of information that, wouldn't you say, Donald? And I know you'll also be interested to learn, just in case you might 'ave forgotten or not been aware, that the said Mr Shelby was one of your predecessors … as school cricket captain. Mr Shelby says the car was stolen while 'e was at the cinema and 'e 'as witnesses to verify that at the time McCarthy was killed 'e was three miles away. This, of course, is being checked.

'Now to the other unfortunate 'appenings. George 'Eritage. Absolutely no evidence whatsoever. From the position of the body 'e could not 'ave fallen more than thirty feet. Could 'ave been less. But 'e was unlucky by all accounts. Banged 'is 'ead on 'itting the stony ground, extensive damage to the brain tissues, and Bob's Your Uncle. At least, that's what they say. No witnesses, no evidence to the contrary.

'Mr Boyd and 'is aeroplane 'as also been recorded officially as an accidental death. Rudder jammed, it seems, 'ardly left the ground and then … whoosh! An inspection of the bits and pieces afterwards showed no signs of anything 'aving been tampered with and Mr Boyd will 'ave to join up in 'Eaven with all those who could 'onestly say it just 'adn't been their lucky day. And Mr Moonsong. Now there is a funny thing. For the last couple of nights, I've taken myself off to the Archduke Ferdinand, just for a drink and a chat, you understand. And last night…'

Mr Chrimes' latest revelation was interrupted here by the entrance from the kitchen of Mrs Margerison.

'Ah, dear lady!' he exclaimed as he rose smartly to his feet, showing no sign of the disorder which had rendered him chairbound only two days earlier. He took off his bowler, hooked his umbrella over his arm, and reached eagerly for her hand. 'I was right, Donald, wasn't I? A beauty if ever I saw one.'

Roseanne giggled like a girl and asked if he would like tea. Mr Chrimes, still clutching her hand, refused, saying he was just about to leave, important call, but another time he'd be ''ighly delighted.'

When Roseanne had managed to tear herself away, Mr Chrimes remained standing, grasping the umbrella with both hands as he continued.

'As I was saying, Donald, I was at the Archduke Ferdinand last night when I got chatting to this 'ere man 'oo 'ad been in the pub the night those three struck up their bet. Now, according to 'is ears, Mr Moonsong did not get involved in the argument about 'oo could swim the fastest. Mr Moonsong listened, and laughed at them, but according to this 'ere man, it was just the other two 'oo were getting aereated about 'oo was the fastest. 'E thought it was just a silly argument between the two of them. But 'e says for sure that all three left together, and then when 'e 'eard that all three 'ad been drowned, 'e just naturally assumed that Mr Moonsong 'ad been drawn into the argument, and decided to show the pair of them. Leastways that was 'is ass-ump-tion.'

Mr Chrimes jabbed his umbrella into the

carpet with every syllable. 'I thought as 'ow you'd like to be kept up-to-date, Donald, and tonight I thought I'd go and see Mortimer Shelby 'oo 'ad the misfortune to lose 'is car the night somebody was killed with it. Don't bother to see me to the door, Donald, I'll see myself out.'

Donald did not get out of his chair, and Mr Chrimes, with a flourishing swing of the umbrella, swept through the door and along the hall.

He opened the front door and off he went into the night, his long strides taking him swiftly along the pavement, his arms swinging briskly, his shoulders swinging, too, and his umbrella click-clacking as he jabbed it at the paving stones.

The prospect of looking into a mystery – a series of mysteries – had galvanised Mr Chrimes. The stimulation of a little detective work did wonders for him, and despite his years he set off for the Shelby home at a fair pace. He hadn't a car – 'bad for the digestion' he always said – and only used the local buses when the weather was extremely bad or his arthritis was playing up. There was no sign of the arthritis now as he moved smartly into the wide High Street, through the quiet Market Square and headed for Richmond

Road. He whistled gaily to himself as he turned briskly into Rolden Avenue, only to be stopped in his immaculate stride by two young children, a boy and a girl, who came dashing down the hill.

'Now, now, now,' said Mr Chrimes softly and with a twinkle in his eye. 'Where's the band?'

The little girl looked up at the rather forbidding man, who took off his hat and bent down so she could get a better look at him.

'No band, mister,' she whispered.

'Well, it must be a ghost that's chasing you then?'

The child giggled and shook her head.

'Well, don't be a telling me. Let me 'ave a guess.' He thought for a few seconds. 'The toffee shop's 'aving a sale. No? Well, where's you off to in such a great 'urry then? Shouldn't you be in now? What will your Mum and Dad say?'

'Mum's going to the pub, and Dad's watching Miss World,' said the little boy, seriously. 'We're all right.'

'Well, look 'ere,' said Mr Chrimes. 'If I was to say a few magic words, I don't know, mind you, but some kind old wizard just might put something nice in my pocket for you two. But only, I daresay, if you was to get off 'ome.

Now let's see. "Upsadaisy, don't be lazy, Quick as a rocket, What's in my pocket?"'

The girl giggled, then slowly put her hand into Mr Chrimes's overcoat pocket. 'Oooooooo!' she exclaimed, and brought out two bars of chocolate.

'Amazing,' said Mr Chrimes. ''Ow amazing.'

He gave the children the chocolate and as the girl took hers she gave Mr Chrimes a quick kiss on the cheek. 'Thank you Mr Wizard,' she whispered.

Both children set off running back up the hill, followed by a shout from Mr Chrimes. 'Don't forget. Straight 'ome.'

After seeing Mortimer Shelby, Mr Chrimes paid two more visits that night before returning home, and in all he reckoned he must have walked ten miles. His first was to pay respects to Margaret Moonsong, widow of Jeremy, his second a return visit to Mr and Mrs Margerison, who were just settling down to a gruesome-looking documentary on brain operations when they were interrupted by a loud knocking at the front door. The noise startled Roseanne.

'Goodness, not again,' she said.

Mr Chrimes was glowing after his long, brisk walk in the cold evening air. His skin was flushed and his eyes shone brightly as he accepted the invitation to sit down. Clearly, he had learned something important, and he could not contain his excitement.

''Ave I got news to impart to you,' he boomed over the noise from the television set, which Donald immediately switched off.

'Mortimer Shelby and I spent a good while talking over old times,' Mr Chrimes began. 'A very interesting experience, you know, going over the days spent at school, recalling the boys you knew, and the men 'oo taught you subjects you 'aven't given a thought to in years.'

He stared into the fire, his chin resting on the top of his umbrella as he recaptured something of his youth. For a moment it was an effort to resume his story, and it was only a bout of coughing and spluttering from Donald that brought him back to his story of the visit to Mr Shelby.

'As I was saying afore I so rudely interrupted myself.' He beamed at the couple. 'The time when Mr McCarthy was 'it was easily fixed at a 15-minute period, that being the gap between 'im leaving the public 'ouse and being found dead at the side of the road. Or to be more precise, draped over an 'awthorn 'edge. Now then, that same evening, Mr Shelby 'ad been to the cinema with three friends of 'is, after which 'e was driven 'ome. Well, not quite 'ome, but to a suitably convenient spot on the main road from which 'e 'ad only a five-minute toddle to 'is 'ouse. Now then, 'e reckons 'e was dropped off at about ten to eleven, noticed as 'ow 'is car, which 'e 'ad left outside the 'ouse, was missing when 'e arrived 'ome a few minutes later, but didn't make a fuss because 'e thought maybe the wife was using it. Unknown to 'im, 'owever, Mrs Shelby 'ad gone to bed early with a bad 'ead, and was fast asleep. All very convenient, you might say, for it was over an 'our before Mr Shelby realised, wakened 'er, then reported 'is car missing, stolen.'

Donald sat spellbound through the story. 'And what time was Ray McCarthy killed?' he asked.

'Well now,' said Mr Chrimes, lifting his umbrella and pointing it menacingly at Donald, 'it's funny as 'ow you should ask. For it was ten past eleven when 'e left the Red Lion, five and twenty past when 'e was found. Ample time for Mr Shelby to 'ave covered the two or three miles from 'is 'ome, sent Mr McCarthy flying, dumped

60

the car, and returned 'ome before phoning the police.'

'But why would he want to kill...?'

'Ah, there's the 'ole crux of the matter,' declared Mr Chrimes, pointing his umbrella again. 'And 'oo knows? Not me as yet, that's for sure. On the other side of the coin, though, I must say I 'ave been told by my friends at 'eadquarters that as well as Mr and Mrs Shelby's fingerprints on the car, another set was found on the driver's door, apparently when it was closed. Nobody else drives the car and the other prints 'ave not been matched.'

'But they...' started Donald.

'And I must say,' continued Mr Chrimes, raising his umbrella and his voice at the same time to demand silence, 'in all fairness to the former 'Ead of Languages that 'e seemed most genuine to me. It was 'ard to see 'im as an 'it-and-run driver. But, 'aving said that, I will pursue this line of enquiry. You can rest on me, Donald. Incidentally,' he added in a tone that suggested that his next remark was anything but incidental, 'did you know a young gentleman called Edgar Richmondforth when you were at school?'

'Edgar! Goodness, haven't seen him in

61

years. Haven't heard of him since Heaven knows when. We were at junior school together and he was one of those unfortunate children who was bought everything three sizes too big for him so they would last him a year or two. Went down south if I remember, Gloucestershire way I think. Old Shelby brought him up, did he?'

'That's quite correct. 'E did. 'As a brother down there 'oo'd sent 'im a cutting from the local paper. Quite a local celebrity it seems, your Edgar. A councillor with all sorts of interests, on the Cancer Research Committee, chairman at the rugby club, captain of the cricket club.'

'Is that right?' asked Donald, excitedly. 'Well, good for Edgar. It couldn't have happened to a nicer chap. A good cricketer, too, good batter. Went in middle order and he really could whack it. And what's Edgar been doing then, to warrant Mr Shelby's brother sending him a cutting?'

Mr Chrimes' back, which had looked perfectly straight as he perched on the end of the seat, stiffened perceptibly. He stroked his chin, then ran his hand smoothly along the umbrella handle as he replied: 'Dying, Donald. 'E's been dying.'

'How ... oh no!' The realisation hit

Donald almost right away. 'Not another,' he whispered. 'How?'

'An accident it seems,' said Mr Chrimes matter-of-factly. ''Ad the 'ouse to 'imself for the day about three weeks ago, and decided to saw a tree 'e'd chopped down into logs. Must 'ave slipped. Cut an artery and bled to death!'

SIX

'And do take your ... your ... accessories ... off my desk, Chrimes, there's a good fellow.'

Mr Chrimes removed his bowler and gloves from the corner of the superintendent's desk, but left the umbrella perched on the edge. He tapped the top of his hat and said: 'Of course. If that is what you wish, Mr Thornton. Only too 'appy to oblige. No offence meant I'm sure. But begging your pardon, I would like to point out that I am no longer a member of the police force, 'aven't been for some years, and that I am now a common or garden member of the public. And 'ow I can recall your words about the members of the public, Mr Thornton... "Whether we like it or not," you used to say, "they are 'ere to stay and we've got to put up with them. By far the biggest majority will come 'ere with the ultimate in preposterous, ridiculous enquiries. But we shall meet them all with a smile and courtesy." "Courtesy," you used to say, Mr Thornton, "costs nothing." So if it isn't a asking too much, I'd be much obliged if I could 'ave my proper tag as a member of the public, a male member of the preposterous public ... Mister.'

Mr Chrimes, sitting bolt upright on the front half of the visitors' stand chair in the superintendent's office, smiled warmly at his former boss.

'Now look here, Chrimes...'

'Courtesy costs nothing, Mr Thornton. Nothing!'

'You come in here about some cock and bull story and just because you're a former member of this Force you think you have some privileges that don't attach to the general members of the public. That being so, do not expect the courtesies.'

Mr Chrimes was still smiling, his hands clutching his bowler hat which contained his gloves.

'Now now, Mr Thornton. I 'aven't come 'ere expecting anything. I've come 'ere with what I think is a reasonable request, for you to consider an investigation into a remarkable sequence of deaths. No. I 'aven't really asked for that. I 'ave done no more than point out to you that the long arm of coincidence seems to 'ave reached out much farther than is natural in the deaths of five former members of our old school. Even if I wasn't a former member of this Force, I would be 'ere as a member of the public, or part of a bond we 'ave in common ... Old Boys of the same school.'

'You were a bit before my time, I think,' said the superintendent, pompously. 'We had little in common.'

'Did we not play in the same Old Boys cricket team a time or two?' asked Mr Chrimes. '*And* against these very boys as I've been talking about.'

'Maybe so, maybe so,' Mr Thornton replied, waving his hand about impatiently. 'But as I have already told you, and as I am perfectly sure you were already well aware, all these deaths have been thoroughly investigated, and apart from the hit-and-run, which could also have been an accident, there is no suggestion of foul play in any of them. Coincidence is a very funny thing, but it does happen you know, Chri...' He stopped himself, then blustered on. 'It does happen, of course it does, you know it does.'

Mr Chrimes sighed deeply, bent his head and looked at the superintendent from beneath raised eyebrows.

'Not a witness to any death,' he said slowly. 'A series of ... accidents ... but nobody saw any of them. What about this last one, Edgar Richmondforth? A regular do-it-yourself man, it seems, a man accustomed to sawing, yet the day 'e gets it all wrong, and cuts open an artery, there's nobody there.'

'His family were out for the day,' explained the superintendent with an air of exaggerated patience. He studied the ceiling as he continued: 'He had felled some trees and was cutting them for logs when the accident happened. This particular, unfortunate tragedy was not in my domain, but I know the officer in charge, who dealt with the matter with the same thoroughness I would have shown myself.'

Mr Chrimes smiled faintly, but listened carefully as the officer went on.

'The body has been subjected to a post mortem and a careful inspection, and there is no question that the saw he was using was the one which slashed the artery. There are no finger prints on the implement other than those of the deceased, no foot prints, no signs of trespassers, no motive, no money stolen, no reason as far as hours of careful investigation have revealed for the man to have been murdered or to have committed suicide. In fact, Chri ... in fact, no nothing! Or to put it another way ... nothingness.

Have I made myself clear? Nothingness!'

Mr Chrimes smiled genially again, leaned forward slightly and rested one hand on the edge of the desk.

'No-thing-ness, Mr Thornton. Precisely. And that is exactly what 'as come out of all the other accidents in the last few weeks. And that alone is very odd, verrrry odd.'

'Odd or not,' snapped the superintendent, 'I have no intention of taking any further action in any case other than the hit-and-run. That is subject to continued investigation and will be pursued exhaustively.'

'Now there's a funny thing,' threw out Mr Chrimes.

The superintendent stopped studying the ceiling and swung round aggressively on his chair to face the older man. 'What's a funny thing?' he barked, petulantly.

'The owner of the car involved in the "accident" with Mr McCarthy was a former Old Boy and teacher at the school, and a member of the cricket team 'imself.'

'I hope you are not suggesting Mortimer Shelby killed this man, then reported his car missing,' snorted the superintendent. 'If you are, I daresay you'll have some wonderful, fantastic story about how he's knocking off an entire cricket team because he was once the victim of a bad l.b.w. decision. It's nothing but a series of coincidences, that's all, Chrimes.'

'But there's five of them,' persisted Mr Chrimes.

'I don't care whether there's a hundred and five,' said the superintendent. 'All five have been checked, carefully, and by experts. Checks that have produced nothing.'

'It's all nothingness and coincidence then,' stated Mr Chrimes as he put on his bowler.

'Precisely,' said the superintendent.

Mr Chrimes had intended returning home for an early lunch after his wasted visit to the police station, but as he was crossing Douglas Road near the supermarket, he changed his mind. He would pay a visit to John Griffin, secretary of the Old Skelhamians, who had retired only the previous month, and who lived alone in a cottage in the old part of town.

Fortunately, Mr Griffin was at home and when the front door was thrown open in answer to Mr Chrimes's urgent knocking, an enticing smell of liver and onions wafted out to remind the visitor that he had eaten only one slice of toast with marmalade so far that day.

'It's Mr Chrimes, isn't it?' Mr Griffin

70

rubbed his hands together in pleasure. Mr Chrimes watched the familiar action of a man who had stood behind the counter at the Co-op Grocery Department for over 40 years, a man who had been subservient to everybody, and master to no one. A modern Uriah Heep. 'What an unexpected pleasure.'

Mr Chrimes stepped inside, drawn by the delicious smell that grew stronger and more inviting with every stride. Forcing himself to forget for a moment his sudden craving for food – especially liver and onions – he asked: 'Do you still keep the old school magazines?'

'Of course. Would you like to see them? They're all upstairs in the back bedroom.'

Mr Chrimes followed reluctantly, loath to leave the delightful smell of food cooking. 'That'll be your dinner,' he suggested, hesitantly.

'Mmmmm, just about ready,' replied Mr Griffin.

'Liver, isn't it?'

'And onions!'

'My favourite.'

'Mine, too! Isn't that a coincidence?'

Mr Griffin's obsequious nature did not extend to sharing his meals, and after showing Mr Chrimes the two shelves full of school magazines, he returned downstairs.

But he was back within half an hour with a welcome mug of coffee and a large piece of fruit cake which he placed on the table at Mr Chrimes's elbow.

'Found what you wanted?'

Mr Chrimes, who had got down to his shirt sleeves, chuckled. 'I've got a bit carried away, to be perfectly 'onest, Mr Griffin. I'm still looking through my own years. Look at this picture of the school cricket team. 'Ere's me.'

He pointed to a thin-faced boy on the end of the back row wearing a cap with circular stripes and a patterned neckerchief knotted at the throat. 'We thought we were the bees knees in those days,' he said.

Mr Griffin rubbed his hands together. 'Every generation of youth thinks the same, Mr Chrimes, wouldn't you say?'

Mr Chrimes enjoyed his dip into the past, and he was over two hours in the back bedroom, skipping through the pages of his adolescence at Skelham Grammar School.

Photographs of the school cricket team particularly interested him. He found the one with Mortimer Shelby as captain, a team that also included a boy who had risen to become a member of the Cabinet for a

Conservative Government. It was when he found the team that included a youthful Donald Margerison that he paid special attention, carefully studying the players and the scorecards of the important matches. He took time over the matches between the school and the Old Boys, and took a note of the scorecard in one particular year. When he had finished, he sat back and looked at it again.

'It's unbelievable,' he muttered to himself. 'Ruddy unbelievable.' He checked it again. 'Crimes! Young Donald's never going to believe this. Not in a 'undred years!'

Mr Chrimes ate a hearty tea. He was ready for it, and after the torments he had suffered at John Griffin's home, he could think of nothing better or more satisfying than liver and onions, with mashed potatoes and peas. He had time for a doze, too, in front of the fire, before he again attired himself in all his splendour and set off once more for the Margerisons.

Donald wasted no time when he heard the robust knocking. He dashed into the passage and immediately recognised his visitor through the glass of the vestibule door by the dark outline of the wide, angular shoulders, the long head, and the rounded finish provided by the bowler.

'Evening, Donald,' greeted Mr Chrimes as he stepped past him and walked straight to the living room. 'And where's your good lady?'

Donald was still at the front door when the question was thrown at him. 'At her mother's, Mr Chrimes,' he called, hastening along the passage.

'Good, good,' said Mr Chrimes, who had already laid his accessories on the table and was in the process of removing his overcoat. ''Aven't I got some interesting information for you, Donald! We'll 'ave to draw up a plan of campaign tonight, and it's just as well as 'ow your good lady 'as gone a visiting.'

He held out his coat to Donald, and took the notebook he had used at John Griffin's out of his jacket pocket. Donald returned from the passage where he had hung Mr Chrimes's overcoat, hat and umbrella, only to find his visitor seated at the table flicking over the pages of the notebook with one hand, and holding out his jacket with the other. Donald scuttled back into the living room and took the jacket which he folded over the back of an armchair. By the time he had seated himself at the table across from Mr Chrimes, who was flushed from the energies of his walk, the desired place in the notebook had been found.

'I went along to see Superintendent Thornton today, Donald,' started Mr Chrimes. 'I 'ad no more luck than you. Dismissed it all as coincidence and ... what was it now, what was the word 'e used? ... oh, yes. Nothingness. Coincidence and nothingness. Anyway, I decided to pop along to John Griffin. You might remember 'im. Worked for the Co-op for long enough, and 'e's secretary of the Old Boys. Keeps all the school magazines from the year dot and allowed me to spend what I can only describe as an 'appy 'our or two delving into them. And it was this afternoon, Donald, that whatever little, lingering doubts I might 'ave 'ad about this 'ere strange affair, were completely cast away. You won't believe what I discovered this afternoon, Donald, not in a 'undred years, you won't.'

He sat back, enjoying the look of excitement and anticipation on the younger man's face. Donald felt his heart starting to beat faster. His throat was drying and he could only croak: 'What was that, Mr Chrimes?'

But Mr Chrimes was not quite ready to

divulge his secret. He continued with the build-up.

'If we are to take it that somebody, some-where, 'as killed off these five unfortunate gentlemen, and if we are to take it that the link with all of them is that they played together for the school cricket team, then we 'ave to ask ourselves, not only why ... but which cricket team is 'e, in fact, getting rid of. I did 'ave a look through the magazines and I couldn't find any record of them 'aving been together in the second team. Now then. Remember telling me as 'ow Matt Thornton recalled playing against George 'Eritage in the Old Boys versus the school match? Told me about it as well, this morning, 'e did. Bowled 'Eritage first ball, 'e did, the jammy beggar. Anyway, when I went through the magazines around this period, I found that the said George 'Eritage only ever played twice for the school first team, one of them against the Old Boys. That same match old Super-Duper was talking about. And that game, Donald my boy, was the only one in which all five played together. SO ... 'ere I was with the five men, all met mysterious deaths, all played together just the once in the school cricket team. And that against the Old Boys. And just guess 'oo was in the Old Boys team that day?'

Donald shook his head. Mr Chrimes was clearly several steps ahead of him and this was no time for guessing games.

'Well, M. L. Thornton, now superintendent, was one, of course. But 'oo else do you know, almost intimately so to speak, 'oo was an Old Boy and a cricketer?'

Mr Chrimes leaned back and his face split with a broad grin.

'Not you!' Donald pointed.

'That's quite right,' laughed Mr Chrimes. 'Plain J. Chrimes was in the team that day. And we 'aven't finished yet, oh dear me, no. Another illustrious member of that side was … pin your ears back, Donald … Mortimer Shelby!'

Donald looked suitably astounded at Mr Chrimes's revelations, which were not yet over.

''Ere's the scores from the game. Copied them down from the magazine. Brought back a few memories, I can tell you.'

Mr Chrimes slid his notebook across the table and Donald seized it eagerly. Mr Chrimes's handwriting was impeccable. A careful, upright hand, without flourishes and easy to read.

'The School

I. A. Boyd l.b.w. b Bell	64
G. C. Heritage b Thornton	0
J. M. Moonsong c Bearpark b Bell	18
E. Richmondforth st Mocton b Beswick	2
R McCarthy b Thornton	32
F. Williamson c Winter b Bell	26
W. Fleet run out	16
O. S. Smethurst l.b.w. b Thornton	0
L. J. Kenny not out	17
M. L. S. Bebbington c Mocton b Bell	2
D. J. Margerison l.b.w. b Shelby	0
Extras	11
Total	188

Bowling: Thornton 3-46, Winter 0-39, Beswick 1-32, Bell 4-41, Shelby 1-12, Bearpark 0-7.
Fall of wickets: 1-3, 2-38, 3-82, 4-86, 5-122, 6-150, 7-150, 8-173, 9-184.

Old Boys

J. M. Taylor run out	6
M. T. L. Shelby b Bebbington	34
J. Chrimes c Fleet b Kenny	16

L. Smiddy c Fleet b Kenny	36
D. Artingstall l.b.w. b Margerison	12
E. Bearpark c McCarthy b Margerison	5
J. S. Winter not out	6
S. Mocton b Kenny	2
S. Bell c Fleet b Kenny	8
M. L. Thornton l.b.w. b Smethurst	0
H. Beswick b Kenny	0
Extras	8
Total	133

Bowling: Margerison 2-27, Smethurst 1-32, Kenny 5-51, Bebbington 1-15.
Fall of wickets: 1-10, 2-30, 3-76, 4-106, 5-115, 6-121, 7-124, 8-132, 9-132.

The School won by 55 runs.'

'It does bring the memories back, doesn't it?' Donald commented. 'That knock of Dickie Boyd's was a fine innings, and that must have been one of the best performances Joe Kenny had for us – 17 not out and five wickets. Won the match for us he did. I do remember you in that game now, Mr Chrimes. You were out to a pretty good catch, weren't you?'

'That is so, Donald. We looked like getting the runs at one stage, and then we collapsed. There was an incident during our innings, 'appened after I was out. I didn't see it, but there was something about one of our players, Luke Smiddy I think it was, getting a bad decision from the umpire, and making a bit of a fuss. But it didn't finish with that, I'm sure. I 'ave a feeling there was more to it, some bit of nastiness after the game, something very unpleasant. Now what was it?'

He thought for a moment while Donald studied the scores again. 'No, it's not coming back. But I know 'oo will remember. Dear old Sam Mocton. One of the oldest members of the team was Sam, but 'e remembers things as clear as if they 'appened yesterday. Me, I can remember faces, rarely forget a face. Sam remembers events, rarely forgets an 'appening. Yes, we'll 'ave to see 'im, and soon, too. But first, Donald, there's something else about that game, something else that might strike you if you 'ave another good look at that scoreboard. Something extra important that'll flatten you.'

Mr Chrimes left his seat and went to his jacket where he took his pipe and tobacco out of the pocket. 'All right if I smoke?'

Donald didn't look up from the notebook. 'Of course,' he said quickly.

80

While Mr Chrimes lit his pipe and resumed his seat, puffing contentedly, Donald studied the scores of the match between the school and the Old Boys.

'No,' he said eventually. 'There's nothing strikes me.'

'Then let me 'elp you. 'Oo, among the five 'oo 'ave died, was first to go?'

Donald thought only for a moment. 'Dickie Boyd.'

'I thought so. And 'oo followed 'im? Tell you what, write them down. Go on. Boyd first, then 'oo was next to die?'

'Let me think a moment ... it would be George Heritage.'

'That's it ... 'Eritage. Go on then. Put 'im next. Then Moonsong, and...'

'Richmondforth next, I think,' interrupted Donald. 'I know he was the last we heard about, but it does seem he died before Ray McCarthy was killed, doesn't it?'

'I was just going to say that.' Mr Chrimes emphasised the point by stabbing his pipe in Donald's direction. 'So that's Richmond-forth next and McCarthy fifth. That's right, Donald, isn't it?'

'Looks right, Mr Chrimes,' said Donald, studying the list. 'Yes, I'd say that was the right order   Boyd, Heritage, Moonsong,

Richmondforth, and McCarthy.'

Mr Chrimes smiled smugly. 'Now Donald,' he said quietly. 'Now 'ave another look at that scoreboard, especially the school's innings.'

The only sound in the room as Donald turned his gaze from the school batting to the list of men who had died mysteriously was the faint hiss of the fire. Mr Chrimes sucked at his pipe and the smoke drifted lazily upwards, floating slowly and disappearing before it reached the ceiling. The only movement from Donald at first was the slight turning of his head. Then his mouth opened wide into an incredulous gape.

Donald ran his finger down the school scoreboard, and then down the list of dead men. 'It's the same,' he gasped. 'Exactly the same.'

Mr Chrimes removed his pipe from his mouth and carefully placed it on the evening newspaper at his elbow.

'You've got it, Donald. They're being killed off in batting order!'

SEVEN

The two men stared at one another, Donald open-mouthed, his head shaking slowly in disbelief. Mr Chrimes sat calmly, waiting for Donald to recover his senses.

It was an effort for Donald to control himself. He managed to close his mouth and stop his head from shaking, but his eyes were still open wide and staring as he exclaimed: 'I was in that team, Mr Chrimes. Me! In that team.'

'Just think yourself lucky you were a bowler, Donald, 'oo batted so badly you went in last. Thank your lucky stars you weren't a good batter, or you wouldn't be 'ere now, talking to me. *You*, Donald, 'ave a chance. After all, we ought to get 'im before 'e gets down to the last batsman, shouldn't we?' asked Mr Chrimes, his eyes twinkling.

Mr Chrimes had lived with sin almost all his life, a familiarity that might not have bred contempt, but had at least resigned him to its inevitability. Not even a case as strange as this could make him lose his natural good humour and optimism. Donald, however, could not stop thinking of the terrible fate that had already met five former schoolmates and would overtake six more people, including himself.

'What sort of a man would do such a thing?' he groaned. 'It's bad enough to plot to kill so many people, but to do it in batting order! Why, Mr Chrimes, why?' he pleaded.

'That's something we've got to find out, Donald,' said Mr Chrimes, seriously. 'And that's why we've got to be 'aving a plan of campaign.'

'Surely, Matt Thornton will take notice now,' Donald cried.

'Not 'e,' retorted Mr Chrimes. 'That'll be just another coincidence in 'is book. More nothingness for 'is files. No, this is something we'll 'ave to do ourselves. And we'll 'ave to be quick about it, too.'

'We must warn the others!' shouted Donald, jumping to his feet. 'We'll have to tell them, they'll have to leave the area or something. Who's next?' He seized the notebook and jabbed his finger at the School batting. 'It's Fred Williamson, then Billy Fleet, Ossie Smethurst, Joe Kenny...'

'Steady on, steady on,' soothed Mr Chrimes. 'Come on, sit you down again,

Donald, and don't take on so. It might never 'appen.'

'It already has, to FIVE people,' shouted Donald. 'And there's no telling that he'll stick to the batting order!' His face went deathly white as he dropped onto his chair. 'He could decide to start at the end now.'

'No, not 'e,' said Mr Chrimes. ''E's got 'is order and that's the way it's going to be. Get a 'old of yourself, lad, and let's look at this thing logically. First things first, though. 'Ave you got any brandy in the 'ouse?'

'Yes, don't touch it much, but there is some.'

'Well, get yourself a glass before you do anything else, quieten your nerves.'

As Donald went to a small glass cabinet in the corner of the room, Mr Chrimes outlined his plan.

'I'm sure as 'ow you're right about warning these other people,' he said. 'First of all, let's 'ave a look at 'oo's left.' He drew the notebook towards himself and ran the stem of his pipe down the list. 'Next in line, I see, is Fred Williamson, Sir Fred Williamson now, isn't it? This lot will come as a shock to the mighty Sir Fed, but at least 'e 'as enough money to be able to 'ire the entire police complement in the county to guard 'im. Yes, we must see 'im soon. There's no telling.'

Donald arrived back at the table with two glasses of brandy, one of which he handed to his visitor.

'Bless you, Donald,' smiled Mr Chrimes. 'These are big 'elpings, aren't they?'

'You never know, Mr Chrimes, it might be my last!'

Mr Chrimes took a sip of the brandy and said: 'It's no good talking like that, lad, that won't do you any good at all. It's positive thinking that's needed now to sort this little lot out. Now, 'ave a drink of that brandy.'

Donald obeyed, a swift gulp starting him spluttering and coughing.

''E 'asn't poisoned your brandy, 'as 'e?' Mr Chrimes enquired, solicitously. 'Anyway, back to business. Fred Williamson. We know where 'e is. 'Oo's after 'im? Billy Fleet, didn't you say?'

'Yes, he lives over in Lessways. Runs a butcher's shop there, been in the family for donkeys years.'

'Well, that's not far to go, is it? And then there's Ossie Smethurst and Joe Kenny. I'd quite forgotten that those two were together in the school team. That must 'ave been the start of their great love affair, I suppose.'

'What do you mean?' asked Donald.

'Don't tell me you don't know they live together?' said Mr Chrimes.

'Well, I knew they shared in their grocer's shop in the Market Square, but I didn't know they lived together. Are they not married then?'

'Yes, to one another. As queer as a twelve-bob note, those two. I daresay they've been together now for ten or twelve years. Lovely old 'ouse up Marlow Lane.'

'That's a busy shop, Mr Chrimes. I should think they do very well.'

Mr Chrimes agreed. 'One of your old-fashioned type shops that is, where you can still feel a customer, instead of a Zombie pushing a basket on wheels in and out of miles and miles of shelves. 'Oo's this next chap, this M. L. S. Bebbington? Can't place 'im at all.'

'I've been thinking about him,' said Donald. 'I can hardly recall him. I have an idea that he came to live in the area when his education was almost over, so that he spent only a few months at school. He could play a bit of cricket, and he must have been like George Heritage, brought into the side when we were a bit desperate.'

'I only 'ope as 'ow poor George 'Eritage

isn't a listening to you now, Donald. Only got in when you were desperate! Still, this lad Bebbington only played that one match as far as I could see from the school magazines. Bowled a bit, did 'e?'

'Not very much. I think he was only making up the numbers. And I've no idea what became of him. As I say, he was only at school a few months and then I don't really remember seeing him after that at all.'

'Right, Donald. Well, that leads us to you.'

Mr Chrimes peered at him as he refilled his pipe and lit it.

'There we are then. The first thing to do is to see our 'onourable knight, Sir Fred, then contact the butcher and Ossie and Joe. And we must find out whatever 'appened to Master M. L. S. Bebbington. Before we go and see Fred Williamson, I think it might be as well to see if 'e's at 'ome first. What about contacting 'im on that telephone contraption of yours, Donald?'

'Oh. Oh yes, certainly, Mr Chrimes,' stuttered Donald. 'I ... I ... I don't think, though, that I'm quite right up to it. Would you mind?'

'Righto. Can't stand those infernal machines, personally. But this is an emergency.'

The telephone was on a table in the passage just outside the living-room door. Mr Chrimes left the door open as he found the number in the telephone book and then slowly and methodically dialled.

''Ello!' Mr Chrimes bellowed into the receiver when he heard a voice at the other end. ''Oo's that? What? I'm not shouting, madam, you must 'ave the thing too near your ear.'

Listening and speaking were two completely separate functions to Mr Chrimes who held the phone in front of him and looked at it as he bellowed into the mouthpiece, and then quickly transferred the other end to about two inches away from his ear to get the reply.

'I asked you first. 'Oo are you? It's Mr Chrimes 'ere. You're the 'ousekeeper, are you? Well, I want to speak to Mr Williamson! All right, Sir Fred, begging 'is pardon. You what! What did you say?'

Donald watched spellbound as Mr Chrimes rapidly switched the phone up and down, from a point about six inches below his chin to one alongside his ear. Up and down, backwards and forwards, and all the time shouting.

''E's gone where? Scotland on business.

With which lady? Oh. Lady Williamson. I see. And when will they be back? My business, madam, is official, 'ighly secret, and strictly private. So if you'd just be after telling me exactly where 'e is or when I'll be able to get 'old of 'im, I'd be grateful. Tomorrow when? Tomorrow evening? Very good, I'll contact 'im then. And goodbye to you, madam.'

Mr Chrimes took one last, long look, at the telephone as if glowering at the housekeeper, and then replaced it on the receiver.

'Shouldn't we try to contact him tonight,' suggested Donald as Mr Chrimes returned to the table where he quickly swallowed a mouthful of brandy.

'It seems 'e 'asn't left a forwarding address. 'Ousekeeper said it was 'ighly secret and strictly private.' Mr Chrimes laughed. 'The clever beggar,' he declared.

'Hadn't we better see Billy Fleet instead, then?' proposed Donald.

'No, I think 'e's safe enough tonight just as long as Sir Fred's still alive. No, the others will keep till tomorrow. What time is it?' he said, drawing a watch out of his waistcoat pocket. 'The evening's barely started, I see. Just the time for a trip out to Sam Mocton's. You'll enjoy that, Donald. 'Elp you to forget

90

your impending doom. Come on. 'E'll tell us all about that match and I daresay 'e'll know what's become of our Old Boys. Them that's living anyway, eh?'

Sam Mocton was as good as Mr Chrimes's word. One quick look at the scores, and the memories started flooding back, and it was remarkable just how much he could remember once he was underway. He was a small, white-haired man with spectacles and a goatee beard which he was able to twitch. When he was excited, it twitched rapidly as if it had a will of its own.

He greeted their arrival effusively and made them take off their coats before ushering them into the warm, well-lit lounge where he introduced them to his wife, Maggie. 'Wed over 50 years now, Joseph,' he declared proudly as he thrust a large whisky at each of them.

Mr Chrimes told him about the mysterious deaths of the five men who had all played together in one match for the school against the Old Boys.

'I knew, Sam, that if anybody could tell us anything about that match and the whereabouts of the surviving Old Boys, it would be you.'

'There was a nasty little do in that match,

if I'm not mistaken,' said Mr Mocton, once he had looked at the scores. 'Yes, I'm sure it was this game for I know we looked like winning it when Luke Smiddy was batting. He was a good player, Luke, a difficult man to bowl to when he was in form. And he was in form this day, such good form that he looked capable of winning the match on his own. Let's see.' He peered at the notebook for a moment. 'Caught Fleet bowled Kenny, that's right, this was it. Billy Fleet – he's got a butcher's shop, you know, in Lessways – was wicketkeeper, and he took this catch off Luke. Well, I say catch. Luke maintained he had never touched it, Billy Fleet said it had hit the edge of the bat. Only the faintest tickle, but a catch for all that. Anyway, Billy appeals for a catch and the umpire gives Luke out. Luke was as wild as could be about it, said he had never touched the thing and if he had, he wouldn't need any umpire to give him out ... he'd walk. He was a queer old stick, Luke, but always fair. And he just refused to go, said he hadn't touched it, he wasn't out, and he wasn't going. But the umpire stuck to his guns and in the end, Luke *had* to leave. I remember him getting back into the dressing room. His face was scarlet with anger and he threw his bat right across the room. Said it was disgraceful. Not just the umpire's decision, but that Billy Fleet should appeal. He raved on and on about the team and what sort of a captain allowed that sort of bad sportsmanship in his team. Swore he'd never play for the Old Boys again, and he never did.'

'I don't remember seeing 'im any other time than at Old Boys' matches with the school,' declared Mr Chrimes. 'We wouldn't see 'im all year, then up 'e'd suddenly pop, just for this match.'

'That's right,' agreed Mr Mocton. 'His parents were killed in an accident soon after he left school and he took himself off to Scotland. He didn't turn up again for a few years, but when he did, he was a wealthy man. Made his money, I gather, in some nefarious way during the war and then got into plastics in its very early days. Made himself a fortune. He had a sister, an older sister, who was made a widow after the war, and who lived about 30 or 40 miles away. He'd see her and while he was down he asked if he could play in the Old Boys team. I think the first time he asked, it happened to coincide with the game against the school, and ever after that he would make sure he was here for the same game. Then there was that spot of bother and he never came back. I did hear he used to come down to see his sister once in a while, but he never bothered about Skelham again. Don't know what's become of him. Probably still in Scotland, and if he is living I think he'll be approaching 70 now.'

'I'd got it into my 'ead that something 'appened after the match as well,' said Mr Chrimes. 'A bit more unpleasantness involving Luke Smiddy.'

'Now you mention it ... yes, he had a Rolls Royce which was his pride and joy, and somebody had slashed the tyres and scratched the bodywork.' Mr Mocton's beard was twitching vigorously now as he recalled the incident. 'Long, deep scratches all along the side of the car, and the two front tyres slashed. They never found out who did it.'

'That's it, that's it.' Mr Chrimes slapped his hand on his knee. 'I just couldn't get it, but I remember it right enough now. Quite a to do, wasn't there?'

'It all seemed a lot of fuss over something trivial,' said Mr Mocton. 'Whether he was out or not, what did it matter, really? So somebody made a mistake. They're common enough in cricket matches like ours and nobody cares tuppence usually. There seemed a lot more to it than there appeared, I always used to think. Didn't you, Joseph?'

'I missed a lot of it, you know, Sam. I was already out anyway, and I was sitting on the boundary edge. It was a beautiful day, I remember that. I could see 'e was annoyed when 'e was out, but I didn't 'ear about 'is car until later on, in the bar. By then, I was past caring, anyway. It did seem a vicious thing to do, though, to make a mess of 'is car. I wonder 'oo did it.'

'I don't know,' said Mr Mocton. 'Our batting collapsed after Luke was out and the game was over with the players back in the pavilion before he got to his car. So it could, and I only say *could* have been one of the members of the school team. But I don't know. That's too incredible for words.'

'There were one or two tempers lost in that game, though, Sam. No telling what might 'ave 'appened. Do you think anybody in your team could 'ave damaged Luke Smiddy's car, Donald, eh?'

Both men turned their attentions to Donald, who was dozing peacefully after this large whisky, his chin resting on his chest and a sound almost like purring coming from him.

'We'll not disturb 'im, Sam,' whispered Mr

95

Chrimes. ''Ad a bit of a shock tonight, poor lad. Now, you were saying about Luke. Did you think 'e was out?'

'I couldn't say, Joseph. I was too far away. Billy Fleet said he definitely touched it, but I remember asking young Dickie Boyd about it, and he was very embarrassed about the whole thing. He was fielding close to the bat, and I reckon he knew Luke *hadn't* touched it, but didn't want to say anything.'

''E was captain, wasn't 'e, Dickie Boyd?'

'Yes. If he really felt Luke had been cheated out, he should have said so right away and called him back. It was his position to do that. But he kept quiet when Luke was arguing the point and there was nothing more to be said. That was the sort of thing that upset Luke more than the decision. A mistake by the umpire I think he would have taken, but to know there were fielders around him who were cheating was more than he could stand. I overheard him in the corridor after the match telling somebody it was a team decision that forced him out. Maintained there were plenty of fielders near the bat who could have supported him and kept him at the wicket. That's really what got under his skin. It wasn't one cheat who had got him out, not just Billy Fleet, but

96

a whole team of cheats. And now a few members of the school team have died rather suddenly, you say, Joseph?'

'Yes, Sam. They're all accidents bar one, but I thought it worth asking a question or two. All very strange. You said something about an older sister, Sam. Where did she live?'

'I don't know. I did hear she was the only living relative Luke had, her and her son that is, but I've no idea where they were. And that's a good few years ago, too. All part of the dim and distant past, Joseph, it can't possibly have anything to do with today, can it?'

''Ard to say, Sam. If it 'asn't, it's a big enough coincidence to qualify for the Guinness Book of Records. Tell me about the other members of the Old Boys team, will you? I know a few, of course, but I'm 'oping you'll fill in the gaps. One or two in there done pretty well for themselves, 'aven't they?'

'Luke Smiddy for one,' Mr Mocton replied. 'Tell you what, Joseph, you fill those glasses up again while I have a look through the names and refresh my memory a bit.'

As Mr Chrimes obeyed enthusiastically, there came a snuffling and grunting from

Donald, who looked round sheepishly.

'And give the lad one,' Mr Mocton sang out.

'Oh no, not for me, thank you,' said Donald.

'Take no notice, Joseph. Give him another to ward off the ghost of Luke Smiddy!'

'Is he dead as well then?' Donald asked.

'Not that we know of,' Mr Mocton replied. 'Just a little joke.'

Mr Chrimes poured again, Mr Mocton studied the Old Boys team, occasionally tutting and murmuring odd phrases like 'Rest his soul' or 'Another for the Grim Reaper'.

''Ere we are then,' said Mr Chrimes as he carried the whiskies to his companions. 'Three large and lovely 'Aigs. All the best to you, Sam.'

Mr Mocton looked up. 'And to you, Joseph. Now I look at this team I see you and me are among the few survivors still in this country. Let's see. John Taylor, Des Artingstall, Stan Bell, Harry Beswick, all passed away. Eric Bearpark and Jim Winter went abroad. Eric left for Australia soon after the war and built up a thriving industry dealing in farming implements. Jim went to Rhodesia, did well in Government life there, I understand. Which all leaves you and me, Joseph, Mortimer

Shelby and Matt Thornton, who I know you'll be pretty well acquainted with, and the menacing figure of Luke Smiddy. That's five of us. Not much left is there?'

When it was time for Donald and Mr Chrimes to leave, Donald prattled on exuberantly about the qualities of Mr Mocton's whisky, his lovely fire, his great generosity, the power of his memory, the colour of his carpet, his exquisite choice in furniture and curtains, the beauty...

'Do come on Donald, time we was off, 'stead of 'aranguing poor old Sam like that.'

'Not at all, Joseph, not at all. Nice to have you.' Mr Mocton beamed at Donald. 'Both of you. If you'd like, Donald, you can leave your car here till tomorrow, and I'll run you home.'

'Not 'im,' boomed Mr Chrimes. 'Right as a shower of rain, aren't you, Donald?'

'But he has had rather a lot to drink, Joseph.'

'Not 'im. Do 'im good. Anyway, 'e's not got far to go. Take it steady, and 'ome in two shakes of an 'orse's whatnot.'

As Mr Mocton closed the front door behind them, Donald made his way unsteadily towards his car.

'Just get the key out,' he muttered, 'and I'll

let you in.'

'Not me,' laughed Mr Chrimes as Donald got to the car. 'I'll walk it 'ome, thank you very much, Donald. Fresh air will do me good. Take care.'

EIGHT

Donald hurried home the following day, bolted a quick tea, and then hastened to Mr Chrimes's home. It was important that Fred Williamson – *Sir* Fred Williamson now – be warned of the danger he was in, and Mr Chrimes had stressed upon Donald the need for urgency and speed as soon as work was over. 'We must not waste any time,' Mr Chrimes had impressed on Donald. 'The sooner we're there the better, and if we're too early, we'll just 'ave to wait.'

It was windy, and the leaves were scurrying and gathering on the path as Donald walked up to the front door. Knocking did not produce a reply, so he again made his way round the side of the house. It was dark, but a lamp, shining dimly on the small table in the sun lounge, lit up Mr Chrimes as he dozed peacefully in his armchair. Again, Donald was struck by how old Mr Chrimes looked when he rested, and it was an effort for him to break into the peace and waken the former policeman. Donald tapped on the window of the door. The cat, startled by even such a faint noise, let out a piercing cry and again leapt from his owner's knee. Mr Chrimes was slow to come to, stirring sluggishly before opening his eyes and responding to Donald's call at the door.

'Come in lad, come in. I'm sorry I kept you standing there. I must 'ave dropped off.' He flopped back into his chair once Donald was inside, and took out his pipe. 'Pass us that mug, Donald, will you?'

Donald slid the mug holding the false teeth across the table and watched fascinated as Mr Chrimes reached in, shook the teeth, then appeared to swallow them.

'Shouldn't we be off, Mr Chrimes? We've got to warn Fred Williamson, haven't we?'

'I just can't 'urry after a sleep,' said Mr Chrimes. 'Takes me time to come round and get my bearings properly. I 'ave dizzy dos if I move around too quickly. Soon be right.'

He lit his pipe, and gave his braces a hitch.

'Don't want me dropping dead on you, Donald, do you?'

Donald smiled, wetly.

'Anyway, I've a piece of information to pass on first, before we set off. I got a few addresses from John Griffin. Billy Fleet's for one, and the last-known address of Luke

Smiddy. It was Scotland, near Inverness, but it was 25 years ago, so there's no telling whether or not it's the same. Still, that's something for me to check later. I also got the last address of that lad playing 'is only match in the school team. Bebbington, wasn't it? That's not far away, so that'll be easy to check.'

'He hasn't been around recently, either, has he?'

'No. Like Luke Smiddy, 'e's 'ardly been 'eard of from that day to this. Of course, as you said, 'e only appeared at school for a few months.'

'I was trying to think of his first name,' said Donald. 'Malcolm, I think it was.'

'Quite a few names, 'adn't 'e?'

'Yes, three initials.'

'And me a plain Joseph, like my father, and 'is father before 'im, and 'is father before 'im. It seems an old-fashioned name now, doesn't it?'

'I suppose it is,' said Donald. 'You don't see children being christened Joseph these days.'

'I always think to the Bible, though. One of the most famous men in the Bible was Joseph. Just as Biblical as Noah, or Peter or John.'

'I like Nicodemus myself,' said Donald.

'Do you?' mused Mr Chrimes. 'Well, everybody to their own taste, I always say. Talking about taste, I 'ave 'eard that Mortimer Shelby's wife 'as quite a taste for other men. She's a good deal younger than 'e is, and not the sort of woman to be tied to the 'ouse by 'er apron strings, so to speak.'

'What does that mean then?' enquired Donald.

'I don't really know. But I still 'aven't been entirely convinced that the 'it-and-run was something Mr Shelby knew nothing about.'

'But if he did kill Ray McCarthy by knocking him down with his car, he's got to be responsible for *all* the deaths,' Donald maintained. 'It really would be too much of a coincidence for him to have killed him in isolation, and yet fitted in perfectly to the murderer's plan.'

'I'm sure you're right,' Mr Chrimes agreed. 'Yet it's another remarkable coincidence that the murderer should pick, quite accidentally, a car belonging to a man 'oo also played in that infamous match.'

'The murderer could have done it by design, purposely drawing attention to Mr Shelby,' suggested Donald.

'Could be, could be. Anyway, we'd best be

off to Sir Fred's. Give 'im the chance to alert 'Er Majesty's Forces and 'ave 'is mansion guarded by troops one 'undred deep.'

It was about this time that Sir Fred and Lady Edna arrived at their home, Marston Hill, after a highly unsuccessful business trip and a particularly trying journey on the motorway.

'It seems to me they save all the work that needs doing on that blasted motorway till they know I'm going on it,' said Sir Fred tetchily as he turned into the drive.

'Do you really think they find out when you're on the road before starting work?' asked Lady Edna, derisively.

'I know one or two on that Board, don't forget, and it wouldn't surprise me in the least.'

'I see. Scores of men are just sitting around on bulldozers and in lorries, with shovels and warning cones at given places all over the country, just waiting for the word that the great Fred Williamson has taken to the road.'

Fred Williamson rarely listened to his wife when he was in this mood. He simply wanted to sound off, and it was always much more satisfying when there was somebody there to shout at. Once inside the house, he picked up where he had left off.

'I swear if it happens again, I'll follow the adverts and go by bloody rail,' he snapped.

'Nobody would see you in your lovely Rolls Royce then,' said his wife.

Her cynicism was lost on her husband. She knew he would never go by rail when he had the opportunity to thrust the ultimate in status symbols at so many people.

'What's the use of having a bloody Rolls, I'd like to know, on roads like these,' he snarled. 'And when some fool isn't blocking them with roadworks, another fool keeps us down to 70 miles an hour!'

'Then why don't you get a Mini? They'll do seventy.'

'A Mini? For me, in my position! A Mini? I wouldn't even let you drive one of those.'

'Then get a chauffeur if driving is always going to leave you as bad-tempered as this. Sit back with your pink gin and The Times and ignore the roadworks.'

'I don't want a chauffeur. I enjoy driving,' he barked.

Lady Edna shrieked in amusement at the illogicality of the remarks. Sir Fred could see nothing to laugh at.

'Give me a whisky, will you?' he said.

'Have your legs and arms seized up with

the stresses and strains those nasty men on the motorway repairs board have put in your way?'

'Of course not.'

'Then the whisky is where it always is. Behind you.'

Before Sir Fred could find a suitable retort, they heard a deafening rat-a-tat at the front door.

'What the hell's that?' he barked.

'Sounds like a motorway man come to get you,' his wife replied. 'I wonder if he's brought his shovel as well?'

The door to the lounge was opened a few moments later by the housekeeper, Mrs Muldoon. 'Begging your pardon, sir, that Mr Grimes I was telling you about who telephoned last night, he's here.'

'Didn't you tell him I had just arrived home, Mrs Muldoon, after a very tiring day. He will have to ring and make an appointment with Miss Yerby.'

Mrs Muldoon respectfully left the room, but was back within a few seconds.

'Begging your pardon sir, I'm sorry I'm sure, but he's very insistent. Told me to tell you it was a matter of life and death.'

'Whose life, Mrs Muldoon?' he asked, tiredly.

'Yours sir.'

'Mmm, it *is* the men from the motorway,' said his wife.

'All right, Mrs Muldoon,' sighed Sir Fred. 'Show them in.'

'Not in here dear,' said his wife in a bored voice.

Sir Fred looked at her in disgust, then rose from his chair and followed the housekeeper into the large, six-sided hall. There were two men. The larger, an umbrella over his arm, his gloves and bowler in one hand, stepped forward, his hand outstretched.

'Fred! 'Ow are you?'

Sir Fred did not offer his hand, but Mr Chrimes seized it and shook it like a bell.

'Should I know you, Mister … er … Grimes.'

'No, not Grimes. A lot of people make that mistake. Chrimes with a C, aitch, as in Christmas. Formerly of Skelham Police Force, Old Boy of the Grammar School, and an old combatant of yours in school versus Old Boys cricket matches.'

'Oh yes, I remember,' said Sir Fred without a flicker of recognition. 'And who's this?'

''Eavens above. Surely you 'aven't forgotten Donald. Donald Margerison, in the same team at school with you.'

'Oh yes, I remember. Long time ago, now. How are you, Margerison?'

Donald winced. They had been on first name or nick-name terms at school, now he was reduced to one of Sir Fred's vassals.

'And what can I do for you? I'm very tired. I've had a very trying journey. My housekeeper said something about it being a matter of life and death.'

'And that's the way it is,' said Mr Chrimes. 'You once played in a cricket match for the school against the Old Boys in which there was a bit of unpleasantness, somebody 'oo thought 'e was cheated out and later 'ad 'is car – a Rolls Royce like yours – vandalised. Do you remember?'

'Vaguely,' answered Sir Fred, with little interest.

'Well, five members of that school team 'ave died in mysterious circumstances and we 'ave no doubt but that you're due to be number six.'

'And how have you come to that conclusion?'

'In the last few weeks, the first five in the batting order in that match 'ave all died. You batted number six that day.'

Sir Fred looked sceptically at Mr Chrimes and then Donald. 'You'd better come in,' he said and turned to the lounge door.

Lady Edna was not one to disguise her displeasure, and Mr Chrimes felt the icy blast as soon as he walked into the room.

'My dear, two former members of the school, Mr Grimes, formerly a policeman, and Margerison. We were in the cricket team together.'

'And what line of business are you in, Mr Margerison?' asked Lady Edna.

'Building society, Mi ... Mad ... Lady ... urrrm, joint deputy assistant manager.'

'Oh yes.' She looked away from Donald to her husband, a clear signal for him to take over.

'They think I'm about to lose my life, my dear.'

'Oh yes. And when is the hap ... unfortunate event to occur?'

'Oh. I didn't ask that.'

'Seeing as 'ow you're next in line, it could be any time now,' said Mr Chrimes. 'That's why we've come to warn you.'

'And how do you think he'll go, Mr Grimes?' Lady Edna asked in a deep, mocking voice.

'Well so far, we've 'ad a climbing accident, a drowning, aeroplane crash, 'it-and-run, and a man 'oo bled to death. You pays your

110

money and takes your pick, madam.'

'It seems, my dear, that five men, all of whom played in the same cricket team as me at school, have died under mysterious circumstances in the last few weeks. Not only that, but they've gone in batting order, too. I'm next man in, so to speak, all padded up, eh, Margerison? So I'm next to go, they say. Presumably, Mr Grimes, the police are aware of this unfortunate set of circumstances. My dear friend, Matt Thornton, has been informed, hasn't he?'

''E 'as.'

'And what does he say?'

'Puts it all down to coincidence.'

'And you don't.'

'Quite correct.'

'Why not?'

'Too many. One or two wouldn't 'ave been so bad, but this is taking coincidence too far. And in batting order, too, without a natural death among them.'

'Very successful man, Superintendent Thornton.'

'And not an imaginative bone in his body,' said Lady Edna.

Mr Chrimes looked at her with a new esteem.

'You get to position of superintendent,

you get to most positions of power, by results,' her husband retorted. 'Wouldn't you agree, Mr Grimes?'

'I would 'ave said there is more than an element of chance in it,' Mr Chrimes answered. 'Opportunity, push, knowing people, right place, right time, they all enter into it.'

'I think he's trying to say that Matt Thornton isn't God Almighty in the Skelham Police Force,' said Lady Edna. 'Men get on more by being pushy, by grabbing, than they do by talents. Ambition can be an occupation in itself. But just because a man gets to a position of power doesn't mean he's worthy of it.'

Mr Chrimes said nothing. Donald shifted his weight on to his other leg and hoped he would not be drawn into the argument.

'Is that what you're trying to say?' said Sir Fred.

'Even Winston Churchill was wrong now and again,' said Mr Chrimes. 'We're none of us infallible. Mr Thornton can make mistakes like the rest of us.'

'But by his position, we can assume he makes fewer than … some of us,' said Sir Fred. 'But it is odd, I must agree, and I will certainly take care when I'm swimming or climbing or doing any of those things that killed off those other men. Now if you'll excuse me, I'm very tired.'

'You did say you remembered the match that resulted in damage to a Rolls Royce later. Can you recall the incident on the field?'

'Not without considerable thought and recourse to the records of the match. Now I must...'

'We do 'ave the scores,' said Mr Chrimes, affably. 'And as I recall, you played a very fine innings.'

'Did I? I'm sure you're right.' Sir Fred looked around as if expecting a ripple of applause.

'Yes indeed,' said Mr Chrimes. 'One of the top scores you were, and out in the most unlucky manner. Quite one of the best knocks I'd seen all season.'

Sir Fred preened himself. It wasn't turning out to be such a bad day after all. What had his stars said today: 'There will be trivial irritations to contend with, but the evening could prove entertaining and harmonious.'

'I was saying to Donald 'ere, on the way over, that I can still remember some of your shots. I don't think magnificent too strong a word to use. Isn't that so, Donald, eh?'

'Oh! Oh yes, yes, quite magnificent.'

Lady Edna looked at 'Mr Grimes' with a new esteem! He had quickly discovered how susceptible her husband was to flattery.

'Well, of course, I was a fine player when I put my mind to it. No question of that. Here, let me see the scores.'

Mr Chrimes reached into an inside pocket and pulled out his notebook. He quickly found the relevant page and handed the book over to Sir Fred, who scanned through the scores.

'Now I remember, yes,' he said. He strutted to the drinks cabinet and poured himself a large whisky, which he topped up with soda. He did not drink right away, but held the glass high in front of him as he walked back towards the two men.

'The stingy old beggar,' thought Mr Chrimes, irritably.

'Times must be harder than they look for Fred,' thought Donald, charitably.

'Oh dear. Curtain up,' thought Lady Edna, miserably.

Sir Fred had forgotten his tiredness. He held the floor in front of two men who had clearly been impressed by his prowess on the cricket field.

'You're quite right,' he said, looking at Mr

Chrimes. 'I did play well that day. Twenty-six runs, but it could so easily have been more. Many more. We won, of course, didn't we? Quite comfortably in the end.'

'Yes. Fifty five runs. But do you remember, there was an unpleasant incident when the Old Boys were batting?' said Mr Chrimes. 'Something about a catch be'ind the wicket.'

Sir Fred took a sip of his drink as he considered. 'Now you mention it, yes I do. Chappie caught by Fleet, wasn't it? Said he wasn't out and wasn't going, but the umpire said he was out, and off he jolly well had to go.'

'Did you see the catch?' asked Mr Chrimes.

'Never a catch in this world,' said Sir Fred, without hesitation. 'I was in the slips and I can tell you his bat was nowhere near the ball. What was the chappie's name, Smith wasn't it, yes Smith, he was right. He didn't touch it.'

'Why didn't you say so then?'

'Nothing to do with me. I wasn't the bowler, the catcher, or the captain. Anyway, we wanted the fellow out. He was going pretty well and we had to get rid of him if we were going to win. And get rid of him we did.'

'But isn't that cheating?' Lady Edna asked, innocently.

'I wouldn't say that,' barked her husband. 'Gamesmanship if you like. But the chaps are entitled to appeal. It was up to the umpire to decide if he was out or not, and he made a mistake.'

'But I thought you said you *knew* he wasn't out,' Lady Edna pressed on. 'Presumably the wicketkeeper knew as well.'

'Of course he did,' snapped Sir Fred.

'And the bowler?'

'I daresay so, yes.'

'Then you cheated him out.'

'Now look here, Edna, you know nothing about cricket. Its rules can be very complex, not the sort of thing you can grasp at all. Not at all.'

'Cheat!' said Lady Edna, simply.

'Umpire's mistake,' bellowed her husband.

Mr Chrimes watched, fascinated and amused. ''E was very upset,' he said in an effort to break up the dog-fight.

'One or two divided opinions on the subject,' declared Sir Fred. 'I know Matt Thornton was bloody wild about it all. Ranted on about the way they were bringing up the whippersnappers at school, these days. Still refers to it now from time to time. Storm in a teacup, if you ask me.'

'There was trouble after, as well,' said Mr Chrimes, who was getting rather tired standing and had taken to leaning on his umbrella as if waiting for the 8.26. 'Somebody made a mess of 'is car.'

'I know nothing about that,' Sir Fred snapped.

'I thought you said you remembered...'

'Well, I don't.'

Donald spoke for the first time, startling everybody with his audacity. 'It was common gossip for a day or two,' he protested. '*Every*body knew about it.'

'Not me!' Sir Fred looked rattled and quickly moved the conversation along. 'I have the cuttings for those matches,' he declared. 'From the paper. I'll show you. Would you mind, dear.'

He turned to Lady Edna, who smiled icily and said: 'Those scrapbooks of yours are rather too heavy for me, dear, wouldn't you say?'

Sir Fred scuttled out of the room and was back within two minutes with a leather-bound scrapbook, beautifully inscribed with his name and date. He put it on the table and flicked through it, skilfully and triumphantly finding it in a few seconds.

'See! See here.' He waved them over perfunctorily, an emperor summoning his slaves. He ran his finger down the two-sentence report on the match which mentioned only Boyd's innings of 64 and Kenny's five wickets in the 55-run victory.

'No mention of me in there,' he said, hurt.

Mr Chrimes and Donald stood behind, waiting for a chance to see the report. Lady Edna draped herself on the couch and looked suitably bored.

'You're wrong about one thing,' said Sir Fred, after another quick look at the newspaper cutting.

'What's that?' asked Mr Chrimes, leaning forward.

'You've come to the wrong man.'

'I don't follow.'

'It's Fleet you should be seeing, not me. Look here.'

Mr Chrimes looked at the point in the cutting where Sir Fred was pointing.

'I wasn't number six that day. Fleet was six, and I went in seven.'

'But the magazine 'ad you at six and Billy Fleet coming in after you.'

'Whatever the magazine might say, I can assure you this is the correct version. I should have been six, that's true. I think I

118

always went in ahead of Fleet, but I was caught unexpected, so to speak, that day. There was a great shouting for me, but I couldn't make it in time. Caught with my trousers down, what?'

'So Billy Fleet's next,' said Donald, his mouth opening wide.

'I 'adn't intended digging 'im out till tomorrow, but I reckon we'd better go now,' declared Mr Chrimes. 'Anyway, I'd still be extremely careful, Fred. There's no telling.'

'Don't worry about me, Mr Grimes. I'll be in good company for the next few days. Matt Thornton and I are going to Scotland the day after tomorrow. We've been invited to go shooting and as it's good for business as well, I shall be off with him. So you need have no worries on that score. He's driving, too, so there's no chance of me dozing off and crashing after being drugged!'

In quarter of an hour Donald and Mr Chrimes were in Lessways. But it took them just as long to find their way to Billy Fleet's home in a new bungalow on old farming land.

'Billy? He isn't home yet. Stayed late tonight to get the sausages ready for the weekend. Always does.' Mrs Fleet's brow furrowed. She looked worried. 'He should

119

have been back by now, though.'

The shop was in the centre of Lessways, across from an Indian restaurant which had only just opened. The lights were still on and a car stood outside the butcher's shop. Mr Chrimes dashed out of the car and hammered non-stop on the shop door.

'Come on, for God's sake, come on,' he muttered.

There was no sign of life in the shop and Mr Chrimes quickly decided to see if there was a back entrance. 'Quick, Donald, with me.'

Together the two men dashed round the corner and through a gate that led them into a small yard. Facing them was another door, which was unlocked. Mr Chrimes quickly went inside, and it needed only a glance to show that Billy Fleet was not there, either in the shop or the kitchen through which he and Donald had entered.

'Thank 'Eaven for that,' he mumbled.

'You thought...'

'I thought 'e might 'ave been be'eaded with 'is own meat axe, yes,' said Mr Chrimes.

'But where is he?'

'Well, 'e isn't 'ere, that's for sure.'

Mr Chrimes walked back into the yard and Donald set off to follow him. He stopped when he saw a piece of blue and white cloth caught in the huge door into the refrigerator.

'Mr Chrimes!' he called weakly. 'Mr Chrimes! Here.'

Mr Chrimes returned and followed the direction of Donald's shaking arm.

'Quick, Donald.'

They swiftly pulled back the two heavy arms which kept the fridge door securely closed. Mr Chrimes pulled open the door, then stepped back in horror as the frozen body, held up only by the butcher's pinny trapped in the door, fell with a thud on the floor of the fridge.

NINE

Superintendent Matt Thornton was a cautious driver. His handling of his three-litre car was a fair reflection of a character built on prudence and vigilance. Sir Fred Williamson, on the other hand, had always been headstrong. Audacious, some would have said. Others would have settled for foolhardy. He couldn't do to sit around for long spells, and the car in which he was travelling with the superintendent had hardly got onto the motorway when he started to fidget. He leaned over towards the driver so he could get a better look at the speedometer.

'I don't know why you get a car with such a big engine, if you're only going to crawl along at 55 miles an hour,' he said. 'That's the third invalid carriage that's passed us in the last mile.'

'It's 58 actually,' said Thornton, whose life was run by precision. 'You never travel with me, Fred, without drawing attention to the speed we are travelling and the number and type of vehicles overtaking us.' He smiled and pressed back in the comfortable seat. 'I don't like going fast, you know that. I get nervous. And when you get to my age, it's comfort that counts, not record speeds.'

'I suppose we must all be grateful you didn't want to be a fireman,' said Sir Fred as he smoothed his luxuriant moustache with the thumb and forefinger of one hand. 'By the time you'd got to your first fire, the whole of Skelham would have been burnt down. At least, if you're going on a murder, there's not much can happen to the body in a couple of days.'

'It would go hard,' said the policeman.

'Like Fleet,' said Sir Fred. 'He must have been very hard.'

'It was 20 degrees below freezing in that fridge,' said Thornton. 'You soon start to freeze up in a temperature like that.'

'That chappie of yours, Grimes, he knew something was going to happen, you know. Bloody odd.'

'Yes, you said something about that on the phone. First thing, he is no longer a police officer, and his name, if it matters, is Chrimes, not Grimes. I couldn't quite grasp what you were getting at yesterday. Tell me again. It'll help pass the time to Scotland.'

'This isn't a serial like the Archers, you

know, going on for day after day,' Sir Fred replied. 'I told you, he came to see me the night he discovered Fleet. On about the number of Old Boys at the school who had died in the last few weeks, all members of the school cricket team at the time I played, and all dying under mysterious circumstances.'

'You said something about the batting order, didn't you?'

'Yes. Well, he came to me because he thought I was next in line, seeing the first five batsmen had all died. He was on about that match against the Old Boys when that chappie Smith was given out when he wasn't.'

'Damned disgrace,' put in the superintendent.

'Yes, we've had all that out before, Matt. But it's that particular batting order that's being wiped out and it was only when I pointed out that Fleet had batted at number six that day, not me, that he hared off to Lessways. And sure enough, Fleet was dead, wasn't he?'

'Lessways isn't my area, of course, but I'm told there is no reason to believe it was anything but an accident. The door swung to behind him and automatically locked.'

'That easy! It just swung to behind him and locked! I thought they were fixed with some sort of safety catch on the inside in case of such a mishap.'

'That was an old fridge. Been in the shop since the year dot, and when it closes, it locks.'

'But it was a family business, Matt. He'd been in the trade all his life, in that shop all his life. He just wouldn't go into that fridge with a chance of the door swinging to and locking him in. It's ridiculous. You're not going to gamble with your life as recklessly as all that.'

'Look here, Fred. It's nothing to do with me. That's Parker's patch, and I'm sure he'll look into the matter thoroughly. But he told me that as far as he could see at first glance, it looked nothing more than an awful tragedy, but for all that, an accident.'

'Matt, I batted number seven in that match, and that *does* make me next for the chop. Now that chappie Grimes was proved right for me the other night, and this has got to warrant some investigation, surely?'

'Between you and me, Fred, I have started the wheels rolling. Only two of the deaths occurred in my area, one of them a hit-and-run. But I have got the machine in motion to see if there is anything in all this.'

'But surely there must be?'

'I have heard of bigger coincidences, Fred. And what is the motive for this wanton killing? Not that a man was given out in a cricket match when he wasn't! He hasn't suddenly taken pique against the school team and decided to take revenge. No, no, I can't wear that. It's too ridiculous.'

'Look here, Matt. I don't give tuppence what the motive is. On the face of it I must agree with you, that it's a daft idea. But we don't know the state of his mind, or anything. Perhaps he's gone mad. What I do know is that six have died in the last few weeks, and they all batted ahead of me for the school. I'm next, Matt, and at the moment I'm wishing like hell I'd never played the bloody game.'

'For goodness sake, Fred, relax. Think about the next couple of days and all that huntin', shootin' and fishin'. And drinkin' and eatin'. If anything's going to happen to you, it won't be on Lord Glendale's estate, now will it? And anyway, you're with me. Now you couldn't be much safer than that, could you?'

TEN

Sir Fred Williamson, chairman of Williamson Engineering Company Limited, died the following morning when his brains were blown out by his own gun before he had had the chance to do any huntin', shootin' or fishin'.

The Lochtamman police were happy to find the situation well in hand and in the charge of an English superintendent when they arrived.

'An Englishman, isn't he?' the constable asked his sergeant.

'Ay, but he's no bad,' the sergeant replied.

Superintendent Thornton told the Lochtamman police inspector, Donald Peaver, that he and Sir Fred had left the house ready for the shoot when Sir Fred remembered something he had left behind.

'His gloves, I think,' said the superintendent.

The superintendent walked on, slowly, Sir Fred returned to the house, and a few moments later there was a bang.

'Unmistakable,' said the superintendent. 'Quite clearly a gun.'

He ran back towards the house and at the corner of the building he found his companion ... 'quite clearly dead.' From an immediate, superficial examination, Matt Thornton deduced that Sir Fred had tripped over a stone, the gun had gone off, and he had been killed instantly.

A deeper investigation by the Lochtamman police inspector, sergeant, and constable, revealed nothing to suggest otherwise, although much surprise was expressed over Sir Fred's carelessness. When it was disclosed that the welcoming party had gone on well into the morning, however, there were knowledgeable shakes of the head among the members of the Lochtamman police force.

'We had all had quite a deal to drink,' the English superintendent said to the Scottish inspector. 'You know how it is.'

'Quite so, quite so,' said the inspector, understandingly.

'Another Englishman, wasn't he?' the constable asked his sergeant.

'Ay, they canna take it,' the sergeant replied.

The news of the tragedy was soon public

knowledge in the small township of Loch-tamman, and it was the local reporter, Alastair McDonald, who transferred it to Skelham in time for the evening paper's first edition.

Mr Chrimes feared the worst when he saw the bill posters in town. 'SKELHAM WORKS BOSS KILLED' the poster screamed. He bought a paper, scanned through the report which was the main story on the front page, and let out a gasp when he saw the refer-ences to his own former boss, Superintend-ent Matt Thornton.

It was a cold day, and a hailstorm lashed Mr Chrimes as he walked quickly towards the office of the Rackington Building Society where Donald Margerison worked. His entrance was as rampageous as the weather. He threw open the double swing doors like Wyatt Earp entering the saloon, then shook his umbrella violently, spraying Molly and Anne behind the counter.

'What a day, what a day!' he exclaimed as he dripped his way to the counter. 'Now then young woman,' he said, choosing Molly because of her looks, 'I've come to see Mr Margerison.'

At that moment Mr Chrimes spotted Donald at the other end of the long room.

'There 'e is,' he shouted. 'Donald! DONALD! Over 'ere.'

The entire office turned to the counter to look at the strange man in the bowler who was waving his umbrella frantically, spraying water everywhere as he tried to catch Mr Margerison's attention. Despite his years, Donald was still able to blush with embarrassment, and he quickly made his way to the counter to make sure Mr Chrimes did not disrupt the office any more. Mr Jenkinson would definitely not like it.

''Ave you 'eard?' Mr Chrimes bellowed when Donald was still only halfway across the room.

Donald broke into a run, his fingers to his lips in an effort to quieten the boisterous Mr Chrimes.

'Sir Fred's dead now!' Mr Chrimes exclaimed as Donald approached the counter.

All heads were still turned towards the eccentric man at the counter and Donald quickly steered him to the nearby interview room. Mr Chrimes thrust the newspaper at Donald who read with horror the description of the death of a man he had been to see less than 72 hours earlier.

'Number seven,' Donald croaked.

'Now in 'eaven,' said Mr Chrimes. 'Things

are moving quicker than I expected, Donald. And 'ave you seen 'oo was with 'im at the time of 'is demise?'

'Matt Thornton.'

'Which reminds me of something I forgot to tell you the other day, Donald. Something which didn't seem all that significant at the time. You remember me telling you there were a set of fingerprints on Mortimer Shelby's car – the one that knocked Ray McCarthy down – and the police 'adn't discovered 'oose they were?'

Donald nodded.

'Well, they turned out to be Superintendent Thornton's! The prints of all policemen in Skelham are kept in case of carelessness. No use 'unting the country, trying to match prints, when all it is, is a fool of a policeman who might 'ave forgotten the rules. I could 'ave understood it of a new detective, a boy on 'is first case, forgetting. But a Super! And old Super-Duper 'imself. 'E was on the case, and it was 'e, apparently, 'oo opened the door before the print boys got there. And now, the same Matt Thornton is on 'and for the killing of Sir Fred Williamson. We've got to move with great 'aste now, Donald. You'd better leave work right now, and come along with me...'

Donald was shocked. 'Oh, I can't do that, Mr Chrimes, it's only a quarter to five.'

'But Donald, it's your life that's at stake!' raged Mr Chrimes.

'It doesn't matter. Mr Jenkinson wouldn't allow it. He wouldn't like it at all. Not at all. It might be different if my mother was dying or something. But not this. Oh dear me no.'

Mr Chrimes could see it was no use arguing. Donald was clearly in greater awe of Mr Jenkinson than any raving lunatic who might be killing off an entire cricket team.

'Well, look 'ere, Donald. As soon as you've finished at this in'uman place, get off 'ome. I'll go and see Ossie and Joe, tell them to expect us tonight, and I've also got the address of that lad Bebbington, the number ten in your side.'

'Is he still at the address you got from Mr Griffin?' Donald enquired.

'No. No 'e isn't. But luckily, 'e's still in Gemble. Friend of mine on the Force 'ere, 'e got in touch with a lad 'e knows at Gemble. 'E wasn't at the original address, but it's not such a big place and 'e quickly found 'im on the electoral roll.'

'He was sure it was him?'

'With initials like those? M. L. S. Bebbington. There aren't going to be too many of them knocking about now, are there? So we'd better get off as soon as we can after you've 'ad your tea, Donald, and see these men. I've an errand to go, and Ossie and Joe to see, then I'll get myself off to your 'ouse.'

Donald was in the cellar when Mr Chrimes arrived. Roseanne conducted the visitor to the top of the cellar steps, then shouted down: 'Donald! DONALD! MR CHRIMES. HE'S HERE!'

'Send him down!'

Mr Chrimes carefully made his way down sixteen deep, stone steps and went through the door, which was marked: 'Please Knock Before Entering.' Donald, a keen photographer, had fitted out his cellar as a dark room and was holding up a reel of film to the light when Mr Chrimes entered.

The former policeman looked round the room with interest. 'This is nice and cosy, Donald.'

'My darkroom, Mr Chrimes. I spend a good deal of time down here, and I like to be reasonably comfortable. I've been keen on photography ever since school, and as it's the only hobby I have, I spend a lot of time and money on it.'

Mr Chrimes looked up the chute, origin-

135

ally built to take the coal from the pavement above.

'I blocked off the hole at the top,' Donald explained. 'Light was getting in, and in any case, it was liable to be dangerous.'

On one wall were two iron rings, about four feet apart. 'They were to fasten the coalman to if 'e delivered too much slack, eh Donald?' laughed Mr Chrimes.

'I don't know,' Donald replied seriously. 'I've never been able to work out what they were for. Perhaps something hung from there, but I can't think what.'

'Quite dry, is it?' asked Mr Chrimes.

'Oh yes. No damp at all. I have my own water laid on, of course, for developing and printing. Very handy.'

'Very nice, too, Donald,' Mr Chrimes looked round again with approval. 'I'd like to see you at work, but we really must get going. I couldn't really talk to Ossie and Joe in the shop, they were so busy, but I told them I'd be along early this evening.'

It was Joe who opened the door to them, and they couldn't have got a better welcome if they had come from Littlewood's with a cheque for £500,000.

'Mr Chrimes!' he exclaimed. 'How lovely

to see you. Put the kettle on, Ossie,' he called back over his shoulder. 'He's arrived. And who's this with … it's Donald, isn't it? How fabulous. Come on in both of you. If I'd known you were coming, Donald, I'd have baked a cake.' He dug Donald playfully in the ribs with his elbow, then wiped his hands on his pinny. 'I was just finishing the washing up,' he said. 'You'll have to excuse the way I look, I've hardly had a minute since we got home.'

Joe carefully patted his hair at the back as he ushered the visitors into the living room where Ossie, a much bigger, stronger-looking man, greeted them just as effusively. 'We do love to see old friends,' he said warmly. 'Don't we Joe?'

'We can get the best china out, can't we, Ossie?'

'Oh yes,' Ossie replied, enthusiastically. 'I think this is an occasion that calls for only the best.'

Joe clasped his hands in delight and hurriedly left for the kitchen. Ossie, Mr Chrimes and Donald were soon discussing the old days at school, a conversation interrupted some minutes later by the return of Joe, pushing a trolley bearing cups and saucers, chocolate cake and shortbreads.

'I hope you like this cake, you two,' he declared. 'It's a new line. We think it's delicious, and we hope you'll go for it, too.'

The tea poured, the cake beautifully sliced and placed on plates, the four men sat back.

'Now then, Mr Chrimes,' said Ossie. 'You were saying.'

Mr Chrimes explained, just as he had done at the Williamson household three nights earlier, how the entire Skelham Grammar School cricket team was being wiped out, methodically and swiftly.

'We were at Fred Williamson's three nights ago, and 'e laughed at us. Don't you do the same,' said Mr Chrimes, looking at Ossie, then Joe, then back to Ossie. 'This stopped being a laughing matter a long time ago. You two are next in the batting order with you in particular danger at the moment, Ossie.'

'What are the police doing?' Joe asked. The cup and saucer he had been holding since Mr Chrimes started his story, had started to shake quite violently, and he hurriedly placed it on the small table at the side of his chair.

'It 'as taken a long time for Superintendent Matt Thornton to accept the obvious, but accept it 'e apparently 'as, at last. Though not with much conviction, I'm told, seeing as 'ow 'e 'as delegated just one sergeant and one constable to make enquiries. But at least something's 'appening.'

'Then we'll be all right,' said Ossie, pleadingly.

'Look 'ere. This man 'as killed, already, seven people. Nine if you want to include the two 'oo were drownded with Jeremy Moonsong. 'E knows what 'e's doing and 'ow 'e's doing it, so if I was you two, I'd take all the care you can and not rely too much on the police in this instance.'

'But what can we do?' asked Joe, pursing his lips, and looking round as if expecting the murderer to pop up from behind the sofa.

'For one thing, stay together. Always,' emphasised Mr Chrimes. 'Protect one another.'

'We do that already.'

'Well, do it some more! Look, Joe. Till this lunatic is caught, your life, Ossie's life, and Donald's 'ere, are in serious danger.'

'Should we go away?'

'You could.'

'No we're not,' asserted Ossie, defiantly. 'That'll do no good. We'll stick it out together. There's two of us, and we've dealt with awkward customers before. We'll deal with this one. Anyway, who do you think it is, Mr Chrimes?'

Years in the police force had taught Mr Chrimes the art of discretion when it came to discussing suspects. He had no evidence yet, and in any case, it was dangerous to talk about the people you *thought* might have been responsible.

''Ard to say, Ossie, although I do believe all this 'as something to do with a match against the Old Boys 25 years ago. One particular match when a man called Luke Smiddy was cheated out.'

Ossie's eyebrows lifted at the mention of Luke Smiddy, and he shot a quick glance at Joe, who squirmed on his seat and looked extremely uncomfortable.

'An incident I think you were deeply involved in, Joe,' commented Mr Chrimes.

Donald, as usual, said little, and left all the talking to Mr Chrimes who was more familiar with such situations. But he didn't miss much as he watched, and it was clear that the reference to the match and to Luke Smiddy had opened up an old wound.

'Well, not really,' Joe stuttered.

'You were the bowler, Joe,' said Mr Chrimes.

'Yes, I know, but it wasn't me that appealed.'

'Course you did,' exclaimed Ossie. 'You know damn well you did. One of the worst pieces of sportsmanship I'd ever seen. I told you so at the time, and you've always known my feelings on the matter. Now don't go trying to say it had nothing to do with you.'

Joe, who was still wearing his pinny, looked appealingly at Ossie. 'You know it was all Billy Fleet's fault, Ossie. If he hadn't appealed for the catch, I wouldn't have done. It was just a reaction. When he went up for the catch, I … I … I just followed him. If he hadn't appealed, I wouldn't have.'

'Course you wouldn't,' snarled Ossie. 'So you say now. You knew damn well he hadn't touched the ball. Nowhere near it, yet you appealed for the catch and you didn't even support the batsman when he said he hadn't hit it. I told you then, and I'm telling you now. You got him out by defraud. It was a swindle, Joe Kenny, and never tell me you took five wickets in that match.'

Joe wrung his hands and pressed them between his knees. 'Oh, don't go on at me again, not after all these years,' he wailed. 'I know I was wrong and I've paid for that day time and again.'

Mr Chrimes and Donald didn't interrupt. It would have been like breaking into a row between husband and wife.

'And you'll go on paying for that day,' Ossie barked. 'It was diabolical what you did, you and Billy Fleet, and the captain, that Ian Boyd. You could all have stopped him being given out, but you let him go. Diabolical!' he spat.

'It wasn't that bad,' shouted Joe. 'You make it all sound criminal.'

'Isn't that what it was?' sneered Ossie. 'You were the luckiest man in the world not to go to court for what you did, and you know it.'

'Court?' Mr Chrimes interrupted. 'Court?'

Joe looked at Mr Chrimes as if he had forgotten he was there. Ossie raged on: 'Yes, court! Who do you think it was then, that slashed Luke Smiddy's Rolls Royce? Don't tell me you didn't know. Mortimer Shelby knew, so I daresay everybody else did.'

Joe was close to tears. 'You said you'd never tell anybody if I... You said you'd never tell.'

'You were all upset, weren't you, poor little Joe?' scoffed Ossie, who had moved to the edge of his seat and was leaning across at his friend. 'Poor Joe was upset, and took it out on Mr Smiddy again.'

'You'd have been upset,' cried Joe. 'You'd

no right to say the things you did to me after he was out. No right at all. You wouldn't leave me alone. Even on the field. You said some awful, horrible things. Awful they were. *You'd* have been upset.'

'But why Luke Smiddy?' asked Mr Chrimes gently. 'Why take it out on 'im?'

'I reasoned in my way that he was responsible for it all,' sobbed Joe. 'I was just confused. I just had to take it out on somebody. The car was the easiest thing.'

'Luke Smiddy responsible,' said Ossie, incredulously. 'YOU were responsible. You and that butcher. You should have been summonsed.'

'Did you ever tell anybody, Ossie?' asked Mr Chrimes.

'No.'

'Why not?'

'The whole thing sickened me,' he said, quietening down. He looked across at the pitiful figure of Joe, his hands clenched so firmly the fingers were white. 'Anyway, I couldn't give an old school chum away, now could I?'

'But Mortimer Shelby knew, you said. 'Ow?'

'Very simple. He'd gone to his car and saw Joe coming away from the Rolls Royce.

Confronted him, and Joe admitted it.'

'Then why didn't 'e report it? Why did 'e keep quiet about it?'

'Search me, Mr Chrimes. But you know old Shelby. He's a queer old stick, and no mistake.'

Mr Chrimes couldn't resist a smirk. 'And nobody else ever knew?'

'I thought Shelby would have told people on the quiet, people like you. But apparently not.'

'Amazing, Ossie.'

'Divine providence, Mr Chrimes.'

'Did anything else 'appen at that match, Ossie, anything else that might 'ave been kept quiet?'

Joe looked up, his eyes wet, his face set in misery. 'Wasn't there enough, Mr Chrimes?'

Mr Chrimes decided there was nothing further to be gained from talking any longer to Ossie Smethurst and Joe Kenny, so he said his goodbyes quickly, and he and Donald left.

'I think you could do with another cup of tea, Joe. What about it?' said Ossie when their visitors had left.

'Mmmmmm. I could do with one. Gave me a nasty turn that did.'

Donald was soon chattering excitedly as

he drove towards Gemble. 'Well, well. Fancy Joe being responsible for the damage to Luke Smiddy's Rolls Royce. You live and learn, eh, Mr Chrimes? Now that was a turn-up for the books. Ossie must have laid it on thick to get Joe into such a state. And didn't he turn nasty tonight?'

'I shouldn't think that's the first time 'e's brought it up in the last 25 years,' Mr Chrimes replied. 'I should say Ossie 'as been 'olding that over Joe's 'ead from the day it 'appened. Joe looked as if 'e 'ad squirmed a time or two over that Luke Smiddy escapade. Amazing, though, that word never got out. I wonder why Mortimer Shelby didn't say anything.'

'Yes, I couldn't understand that,' Donald declared. 'Shelby was such a strict disciplinarian, such a great one over behaviour, that this must have appalled him. At least you'd have thought so.'

'Unless...' started Mr Chrimes.

'Yes?'

'Unless ... Shelby used it like Ossie. 'Eld it over 'im.'

'A sort of blackmail you mean?'

'In a way.'

'For what purpose?'

'Well, what purpose would there be with

Joe? 'Omosexuality, I suppose.'

'But there was never any suggestion of that with Shelby, was there? In any case he's married.'

'That doesn't mean anything, Donald. 'E did marry late, you know. And 'omosexuals didn't splash it around in our day the way they do today. None of your gay exhibitionism when we were lads, eh?'

'Do you really think that could be the reason?'

'It's a suggestion, that's all, Donald. Just a suggestion. Per'aps 'e's been getting free groceries for the last 25 years – 'oo knows?'

'Mortimer Shelby for one.'

'You're right there. But it doesn't necessarily 'ave any bearing on this 'ere other matter, does it?'

'But it all happened on the same day, Mr Chrimes. It's the school team that played the Old Boys 25 years ago that's being knocked off, and we do think this Luke Smiddy business had something to do with it, don't we?'

'Yes, Donald, I must say it does look as if there 'as to be a tie-up somewhere with everything that 'appened that day and all these killings. So maybe Mortimer Shelby and Joe Kenny are involved some'ow.'

'All very strange, Mr Chrimes. And all the time the number of people who played in that match is getting smaller and smaller.'

'Yes, only four members of the school team left. Ossie and Joe, this man Bebbington, and you, Donald. Now the Old Boys outnumber you, with Mortimer Shelby, Matt Thornton, Luke Smiddy, Sam Mocton and me. What do you think, Donald? Is there a murderer, a mass murderer, in there somewhere?'

'What about those two other Old Boys Mr Mocton said had gone abroad?' asked Donald. 'There's no chance of them being around these parts, is there?'

'No. We can rule them out. Eric Bearpark, the one 'oo went to Australia and built up a farm implements business, 'e's still going strong and 'asn't been to this country in years. The other one, Jim Winter, died in Rhodesia two or three years ago. I've been thinking, Donald.'

'What about, Mr Chrimes?'

'I think it's time I went to see Luke Smiddy. What 'appened to 'im that day is at the 'eart of this matter, and the sooner I get a word with 'im, the better.'

'But you're not sure where he is, are you?'

'Yes I am. The address is still the same, 'e's

still living, and as 'e isn't on the telephone, I 'ave no choice but to make the journey into Scotland.'

Donald was quiet for a moment. He turned on the windscreen wipers as a few spots of rain splashed on the glass, then said: 'I'll come with you.'

'But what about Mr Jenkinson?' Mr Chrimes smiled, but Donald could not see it in the dark.

'I thought we might go at the weekend,' said Donald. 'I could take the car.'

'Are you sure, lad? And what about your good lady? What will she say?'

'Oh, she'll be all right. Take herself off to her mother's, I should think. In any case, I'll feel a lot safer if I stick around you till this thing is sorted out.'

'All right, Donald. A capital suggestion. And tell you what? If you take your car, I'll pay for us to spend the night at some local 'ostelry in Scotland. I'll enjoy it. I don't do much with my money these days and it'll give me a great deal of pleasure.'

Mr Chrimes rubbed his hands and smiled again, gleefully. A few minutes later they were in Gemble and approaching a small house in a terraced street. There were no lights at the front of the house, but one soon shone through the small glass pane in the front door after Mr Chrimes had delivered a sharp rat-a-tat-tat on the handle. A face appeared at the window, but the visitors were unable to make it out in any detail because of the rain running down the glass. The eyes moved quickly from Mr Chrimes to Donald, then back to Mr Chrimes. Then they heard the sound of a bolt being pulled back. Then another. The door opened.

A man faced them. They could not see him properly from the dimness of the street lamps, but the hall light behind him gave them the outline of a tall, skinny, stooping man with his shirtsleeves rolled up to the elbow. He didn't say anything, but simply stood, looking at the formidable, erect figure of Mr Chrimes.

'Mr Bebbington?' said Mr Chrimes after an interval.

'Yes.' The reply was uncompromising, cold and uninviting.

'My name is Chrimes. Joseph Chrimes. We played on opposite sides in a cricket match long ago. You probably won't remember me, but I'm sure you know Donald 'ere, Donald Margerison, played in the same side with you.'

The man transferred his gaze to Donald.

'It's been a long time,' he said without giving any hint of whether or not he did recognise or remember Donald Margerison.

It was raining heavily now, but the man made no attempt to invite his visitors inside the house. Instead he filled the narrow opening in the doorway and switched his attention back to Mr Chrimes.

'We've come to see you about ... do you think we could step inside? It is raining rather 'eavily out 'ere.'

They followed the man into a room where a black-and-white television set was switched on. A pop group was playing and the loud music reverberated through the room. One bar of an electric fire was glowing faintly and giving off little heat and the only light came from a lamp near the television set. It was a cheerless room. The carpet was threadbare in patches, the curtains had shrunk and did not meet, and the woodwork obviously had not been painted for years.

Bebbington went to the television set and turned down the volume. The picture, however, stayed on.

Donald again played the silent partner. He didn't think he had ever seen a more forlorn face. To start with, it was skinny as if the man was underfed. The brown eyes were dull and expressionless and the weak mouth turned down at the corners. Donald only vaguely recognised Bebbington, and as he looked at the face, sour in repose, it crossed his mind that perhaps it never smiled. Even the man's nose looked unhappy.

'Several members of Skelham Grammar School cricket team 'ave died recently,' started Mr Chrimes.

'If you've come for a donation, I can't afford it,' said Bebbington, whose gaze kept flitting to the television set.

'No. We've come to warn you,' said Mr Chrimes.

Bebbington shivered, then thrust his hands deep into his trousers pockets.

'You think I might be next, do you?'

'Not quite, no. Next but two if you want it exact.'

'Luke Smiddy's decided to take his revenge at last, has he?' Bebbington snapped.

Mr Chrimes stared at him in astonishment. 'What makes you say that?'

A startled look flashed across the man's face. 'I only played in one cricket match for that school,' he said. 'And it's not a game I'm likely to forget.'

'Why?'

'WHY? WHY? You played in it, didn't you?

And you!' he added, turning his attention to Donald. 'You don't play in that sort of game every day, do you? I had nearly finished at school when that game was played, but if I had stayed on I would never have played again. That was the worst bit of sportsmanship I've ever seen on any sports field,' he declared.

'What makes you say that?' asked Mr Chrimes.

'Luke Smiddy was never out in a month of Sundays,' Bebbington said with feeling. 'Everybody knew that except that fool of an umpire, yet nobody said a word.'

'Why didn't you?'

'I was the new boy. It was my first match and it wasn't my place to say anything. Why didn't you?' He rounded on Donald as he flung the last question out and it suddenly struck Mr Chrimes that he himself had not asked Donald. Nor had Donald offered any explanation.

'I was nowhere near it,' Donald blustered.

'*I* wasn't,' said Bebbington. 'But I knew.'

'In any case, I was a bit like you,' Donald went on. 'I was fairly new to the team.'

'If I had been Joe Kenny or Billy Fleet or that weak-kneed idiot of a captain, Boyd, I wouldn't have been able to sleep that night after being party to the worst bit of cheating I've ever seen,' said Bebbington.

'I couldn't see anything to get excited about at all,' said Mr Chrimes. 'Bad decisions are part of sport. You've got to learn to live with them, not go on making a terrible fuss about them.'

'Who's talking about the decision?' Bebbington exclaimed. 'All right that was bad. It's what the players did that's so bad. And there were players there that could have changed that decision. That fellow that was killed today, Fred Williamson, I remember he sneered. Thought it was a real big deal. All he could say was "Good riddance." And what would he have said if it had happened to him, that's what I'd like to know?'

Bebbington was into his stride. The solitary cricket match he had played for the school had made a lasting impression and he poured out all his feelings in front of his visitors.

'And then … then somebody goes and makes a mess of his car. It was unbelievable. A cricket match. The game for gentlemen they say, don't they? It produced all that. I'm not surprised Luke Smiddy went off the deep end about it. Criminal it was, criminal.'

'You left school soon after that match

then?' asked Mr Chrimes.

'Yes, we only moved to the area because Dad had died, and I caught the last three or four months at the school. Rotten school it was as well.'

'You're not married then?'

'Not me. You won't catch me caught with a nagging woman and brawling brats. Like my independence I do. There's nobody will take that from me. Anyway, what was it you said you wanted? Warn me about something, wasn't it?'

Mr Chrimes pushed his shoulders back and stretched to his full height. 'All the first seven players in that school team against the Old Boys 'ave died recently,' he said. 'In mysterious circumstances and all made to look like accidents. Fred Williamson was the seventh, the same position 'e batted in that day. You were tenth in that game, weren't you?'

Bebbington, who had been standing in front of the fire, had moved slightly to get a better view of the television set. He didn't look away as he replied: 'Fancy remembering that,' he said.

'Crimes, lad, I couldn't remember something like that. I 'ad to look it up. I 'ad to find the scores. That's where I got the batting order from.'

Bebbington looked at Mr Chrimes. 'I've got the scores of that match,' he said. 'Over here.' He moved across to a shelf of books and from between the paper-back versions of Room At The Top and 4.50 From Paddington he took out a sheet of newspaper. He opened it out on the table and pointed to the report of the match, the same one that Sir Fred Williamson had produced.

'And you think somebody's killing the school team off?' he declared. 'In batting order? Well, well, well. Of course we don't get the Skelham paper here, so I don't keep up with the news. Unless it's a big name like the great Sir Fred Williamson that is. And all these men are dead, are they?' He ran his finger down the list of names. 'And you think Luke Smiddy's taking his revenge, do you?'

'Did I say that?'

'You inferred it. You used to be in the police, didn't you? What've they got to say about all this?'

Mr Chrimes let out a sigh. 'Not very much,' he admitted.

'Luke's a bit too clever for them, is he?'

''E's a clever man, old Luke.'

'Must be, if he can make a lot of murders

look like accidents. What makes you think they're not all accidents, anyway?'

'They're following too rigid a pattern. And that pattern makes you very close to death, Mr Bebbington. That's why we've come. You've got to be very careful. On the watch all the time. It would be better if you could go away somewhere. Can you leave the area for a time?'

'There's nowhere for me to go. In any case, I haven't the money. I'm a bus conductor, you know, not a plastics mogul. I have to watch the pennies. I'll stop here. Don't bother about me. I'll bolt the door.'

ELEVEN

Mr Chrimes was slow to get moving in a morning. He usually wakened about six and made himself a cup of tea which he took back to bed. Then he would doze and think, and think and doze before getting out of bed. If he was going out in the morning he would shave, if not he would go straight downstairs, and make himself a light breakfast, usually toast and cheese and another pot of tea. He took things fairly easily for he found that too much energetic behaviour early in the day left him dizzy and unsteady on his feet. Consequently, it could be ten o'clock or half past before he was into his full swing, ready for whatever the day might hold.

He rarely got a letter so he had given up looking for the postman. Bills in brown envelopes were fairly common, interesting and inviting letters from person or persons unexpected was right out of the ordinary. So it came as something of a surprise to find two letters on the doormat the morning after seeing Joe and Ossie, and 'that strange young fellow,' Bebbington. One of the letters didn't bear a stamp. The handwriting was printed, childlike, as if the owner was trying to disguise it. The other was much more business-like, beautifully typewritten and carrying a first-class postage stamp. Mr Chrimes took the letters back into his sun lounge and seated himself comfortably in his armchair before opening them. Even then he took his time. He held one in each hand and considered them carefully, savouring them, anticipating them.

He looked at the unstamped one, pushed by hand through his letterbox. Maybe Donald called before he went to work and didn't want to waken him. Or perhaps it was from Billy Clifford, just higher up the road, wanting him to collect something from the market.

The other one looked much more interesting. He decided to leave it till last. He tore open the unstamped envelope and unfolded a sheet of white paper bearing the same immature handwriting. There was no address and no signature. He read: 'I hear you've started asking questions about one or two mysterious deaths that there's been recently. You might like to know that Ray McCarthy had been knocking off Mortimer Shelby's wife.'

Mr Chrimes thought about that. Mortimer Shelby had married late, probably in his early forties, and had created quite a stir by choosing a woman considerably younger than himself. Even so, Mrs Shelby would still be a good deal older than the dead Ray McCarthy, eight or ten years at least. Not that it made all that much difference at that age. And it was Shelby's car, of course, that had been involved in the hit-and-run that had resulted in McCarthy's death. Even so, Shelby was not his first choice as a mass murderer, not by a long way. But if the letter-writer was correct, if McCarthy had been having an affair with Mrs Shelby, then things would look black indeed for the former Head of Languages at Skelham School. Mr Chrimes was certain that who-ever had committed one of the murders, had committed them all. He could not believe that Shelby could have killed McCarthy for revenge, and that the other six had been the victims of somebody else. For Shelby to have killed McCarthy and unwittingly fitted perfectly into the murderer's plan was another coincidence that Mr Chrimes could not accept.

He turned to the second letter. It was from Superintendent M. J. Thornton, curt and demanding. 'Dear Sir, Be good enough to call at this office to see me as soon as possible.' What's bitten him, thought Mr Chrimes. Something's up. Something had obviously put Superintendent Matt Thornton off his dinner, and it looked as if he was going to vent his anger on plain Joseph Chrimes, Esquire. Mr Chrimes smiled and bent to stroke his cat, which was rubbing itself on his shin. 'Mr Thornton can wait a little while, eh, 'Umpty? Give the old bugger time to cool down, I think.'

The skies were almost completely clear after the rain of the previous day, but the morning was cold, and as well as a Shetland wool pullover under his waistcoat, Mr Chrimes wrapped his warmest scarf around his neck before setting out for the Shelby home. The way to keep warm, he had learned on the beat, was to keep everything moving, so he kicked out his legs, swung his arms vigorously, and flexed his fingers as he bustled along the street. He wondered how to broach the subject of McCarthy and Mrs Shelby when he got there. He had had to deal with delicate matters several times in the past and had usually found a satisfactory way of handling it. If not, he found the answer was simply to ask the question outright. Hang the delicacy, and see what bluntness produced. But in those days he had the weight of law and order behind him; today he was a private citizen who could easily be told to go to hell. He was still thinking about the matter when he rang the doorbell at number 236, Richmond Road.

Shelby greeted a fellow Old Boy enthusiastically, and pressed him into a cup of coffee, over which Mr Chrimes mentioned his visit the previous night to see Bebbington.

'A strange bird, 'e is,' said Mr Chrimes.

'I remember him,' said Shelby immediately. 'He was at school for only a short time, but made a great impression on me. Brilliant at French, absolutely brilliant. But he had no thought about going on to university. His father had just died and he needed to go to work now he was the money-earner in the family. And you say he works at the bus depot now. In Gemble is that?'

'I assume so,' said Mr Chrimes.

'What a waste. I have rarely come across a boy with such a talent for a language and where has he finished up? On the buses. Do you know, I was so impressed I went to see his mother to see if there wasn't a chance of him going to university, taking languages. Or at least putting his gift to some use. Poor woman! They had no money at all. She had one source she could tap for the money that would be needed, but that obviously came to nothing. I almost despair sometime when I see such talent wasted, Joseph. His mother wasn't well enough to go out to work full time, so he had to do it, and a great opportunity was lost. He really was quite outstanding, you know. And what made you call on him?'

Mortimer Shelby listened, captivated, while Mr Chrimes expounded this theory.

'That's amazing, Joseph. So whoever stole my car the night Ray McCarthy was killed, has murdered all the others as well? That's incredible. All this time, I thought his death had been an accident and now I learn my car was a deliberate object of death. The weapon by which a man was quite intentionally slain. I won't be able to sit in it again. How awful, how perfectly awful. And what a coincidence that he should pick on my car.'

''Ow do you mean?' asked Mr Chrimes as he reached for another ginger biscuit.

'Well, he chose a car belonging to somebody who had played in that same match you were talking about. That infamous game you now think is at the root of the whole terrible affair. That *is* a coincidence, you must agree.'

Mr Chrimes munched noisily on the biscuit. 'Is it?' he asked.

'Well, the murderer wasn't to know it was my...' Shelby stopped in mid-sentence and stared stupidly at Mr Chrimes who was reaching for another ginger biscuit. 'That's dreadful,' he gasped.

Mr Chrimes hurriedly dropped the biscuit back on the plate. 'Sorry,' he mumbled. 'They're so good, I was quite getting carried away.'

'No no. Please do help yourself, Joseph. Have the whole plateful, if you want. No, you mean you think the murderer deliberately chose my car to run McCarthy down with. But why? Whatever reason could he possibly have...' Again he stopped as another idea hit him. 'I DON'T BELIEVE IT!' he cried.

The shout startled Mr Chrimes so much that as he spun round to see what had upset Shelby, he sent the plate of ginger biscuits flying on to the floor. He bent down to retrieve them and was just gathering the last from behind the leg of an ornate writing table when Shelby found his voice again.

'You think he wanted the police to believe that *I* did it. That *I'd* run the poor man down. But why should I want to do that? WHY?'

Mr Chrimes spotted the opening he had been looking for.

'Did you know Ray McCarthy?' he asked.

'Not really. Taught him at school, of course. I've seen him now and again about town. But I wouldn't say I knew him.'

'What about your good lady? Did she know 'im?'

'Not that I know of. But then, I don't know all her friends and acquaintances, no more than she knows all mine.'

'She could 'ave been acquainted with 'im then?'

'Like I say, I suppose so. But what has all this got to do with her? Whatever does it matter whether she knew him or not. It was *my* car, driven by some lunatic, and all, presumably, part of some master plot.'

'Could she 'ave been 'aving an affair with 'im, Mortimer?' asked Mr Chrimes bluntly.

'Jean? With Ray McCarthy? He wasn't in her league at all. I shouldn't think she'd be seen dead with him. I've ... I've never heard such a thing. McCarthy? He wouldn't know how to behave with a woman like Jean. He'd no class, no style. All noise and boorish.'

'You said you didn't know 'im.'

'What? That's right. I didn't. It's what I've heard. Everybody knows about him, thinking himself the gay man about town.'

'Is that so?'

'Getting off with the women. Thought himself such a clever so-and-so with his airs and graces, his smooth talking. I shouldn't... Why did you ask if he was having an affair with Jean. Who's been saying things like that?'

Mr Chrimes looked down at his highly polished shoes and said: 'There's always gossip at times like these.'

'Well, it's a pity you've nothing better to do than listen to spiteful, malicious gossip like that, Joseph. A great, great pity indeed. You don't know Jean very well, do you?'

''Ardly know 'er at all.' Mr Chrimes shifted uncomfortably on the chair.

'Well, if you did, you wouldn't make statements like those,' said Shelby. 'You did say, Joseph, didn't you, that you're not here in any sort of official capacity. You have completely finished with the police force now, haven't you?'

'Indubitably. Quite indubitably,' replied

Mr Chrimes.

'All this does sound like an interrogation. I was just wondering.'

'Several people 'ave been killed so far, and I don't want any more to go,' said Mr Chrimes, gently. 'Matt Thornton does not seem too interested in a mystery that 'as quite got a 'old of me. There are one or two strange aspects, you see, Mortimer, and I am trying, in a completely unofficial capacity of course, but using my professional know-'ow which took me 'undreds of years to acquire, to get to the bottom of the matter and so save at least four more lives. Everything seems to 'inge, like I told you before, on one cricket match in which you and I, to name but just two, are among the rapidly-decreasing number of survivors.'

'Yes. Quite perplexing, isn't it? You did refer to that incident regarding Luke Smiddy, but you can't really believe the old bounder is working off a 25-year hate in this way.'

'The more I think about this, the more convinced I am that that game, that incident, is responsible for all these people dying. The only other explanation is that something else 'appened that day that we don't know about. That I don't know about, anyway.'

Shelby stiffened perceptibly. 'You're

insinuating again, Joseph! Would you like me to get some more ginger biscuits?'

'That's very kind of you, Mortimer, no thank you.' Mr Chrimes stared the other man in the eye. He could look rather formidable when he adopted this stern pose, and much of the gentleness that was usually so evident in all his questioning left his face as he continued: 'It is not my practice to insinuate. I do not like intimations, but much prefer straight talking. It gets to the 'eart of a matter so much more quickly. That being so Mortimer, let me ask you then, why, on the day we are talking about, did you choose to turn a blind eye to a blatant piece of vandalism by a boy of Skelham Grammar School?'

Shelby, whose attention had been riveted by Mr Chrimes's hypnotic stare, flinched at the question. His eyes opened wider as if he were having difficulty focusing. 'What do you mean?'

'I thought that was a plain question,' said Mr Chrimes. 'Luke Smiddy's car was scratched and the tyres were slashed after the match, and you know 'oo did it, don't you?'

'What makes you say that?' Shelby gasped.

'What makes me say it is neither 'ere nor there now, is it? The only thing that does matter is whether it's true or not. And it is true that you saw Joe Kenny coming away from the Rolls Royce, and when you 'eard that the car 'ad been vandalised, you chose not to report the offender, isn't that so?'

'I made a decision at the time, Joseph, rightly or wrongly, and I will not be held to answer for it now, 25 years later.'

The gentleness had returned to Mr Chrimes's face. The warmth was back around his eyes, his strong chin looked just a little more friendly.

'Look 'ere, Mortimer, you and I 'ave known each other a long number of years. You don't need me to tell you 'ow important that incident is in the light of present 'appenings. Ossie Smethurst knew Joe 'ad done it. I know why *'e* said nothing. But you believed in discipline and order, yet 'ere was a boy 'oo blatantly committed a criminal act, virtually under your eyes, and you protected 'im. It seems important to me to find out why.'

Shelby put his hands to his head, then covered his face. Slowly, his head moved up and down, like a baby gently rocking, and once he took his hands away and opened his mouth as if to speak. He closed it again as if having second thoughts and resumed his pose, rubbing his sweating forehead with his fingers as he rocked. Mr Chrimes waited patiently. He poured himself another cup of tea and waited for Shelby to speak again.

'Joe was a lonely lad,' said Shelby slowly and quietly. 'Apart from Ossie and one or two others he was shunned by the other boys at school. I didn't really feel he had been involved in the appeal that got Luke out. Remember, I was batting at the other end when Luke was given out and it was Billy Fleet who was almost totally responsible for the appeal. Joe joined in late, almost as an after-thought, but it was reaction more than anything. I think he regretted it. Ossie tore into him more than once while I was still batting, and it always surprised me that Joe was able to maintain enough self-control to bowl well enough to get some more wickets.'

'Joe knew Luke wasn't out,' Mr Chrimes pointed out. ''E could 'ave done something to 'alt the injustice.'

'I don't think he knew what to do,' Shelby continued as he gradually regained his own self-control. 'Even at that time he was dominated by Ossie and he didn't make many of his own decisions. So he did what he had always done, left it to others. And one or two

169

others, particularly Boyd and Williamson, senior members of the team, were happy to see Luke Smiddy go. They did nothing, and Joe went along with them. Ossie gave him hell and Joe was clearly in a terrible state when he left the field. When I saw him coming away from Luke's car, he was crying. I just felt so terribly sorry for the lad. He was nearly finished with school and I didn't feel it was necessary to drag him into the courts. So I left well alone.'

'Mmmmmm.' Mr Chrimes had more to say on the delicate subject, but didn't know quite how to pursue it. He fiddled for a moment with the buttons on his waistcoat, then settled again for the plain-spoken approach.

'You got to know Joe pretty well after that, once 'e'd left school, didn't you?'

Mortimer Shelby smiled ruefully. So Joseph Chrimes knew. What else had Joe Kenny told him? But what did it matter now?

'Yes,' he sighed. 'Yes I did. As I said, I was sorry for him. I grew very fond of him actually.'

'I 'ad 'eard,' said Mr Chrimes, as he studied the bottom button on the waistcoat. 'And would you say that your action, or inaction I should say, on the day of the cricket match, 'ad something to do with your later relationship?'

'Now that I would call an insinuation, Joseph.' Shelby smiled weakly. 'I didn't blackmail him, if that's what you mean.'

'No, I didn't mean that. You say you were sorry for 'im. Per'aps he was, shall we say, obliged to you.'

'There was a feeling between us. One of … compassion on my side, yes, maybe gratitude on his. Relationships have blossomed, Joseph, on baser qualities than those.'

'And what did Ossie 'ave to say about all this?'

'Ossie? He knew nothing about it. Our … er … attraction for one another did not last more than a few months, maybe a year, and Ossie, I can assure you, never knew.'

'So Joe was unfaithful, on the quiet.'

'That's one way of putting it.'

'An eternal triangle with a difference,' murmured Mr Chrimes.

'Ossie had quite a temper, believe me. If he had got to know about this, there'd have been murder!'

It was lunch time when Mr Chrimes set off for what was obviously going to be an unfriendly encounter with Superintendent Thornton. He slowed down from his usual pace, almost strolling the mile and a half to the police station where he discovered that the superintendent, in fact, was out at lunch. Mr Chrimes decided to do some of his shopping, and for the next hour he wandered round the stalls in the market square, buying a cauliflower for his tea, and boiled ham and sausages from the cooked meat stall. The boiled ham was for sandwiches on the journey to Scotland with Donald, and he also bought four barmcakes and two oatmeal biscuits from the confectioner's. He took his time and it was over an hour later before he returned to the station.

The superintendent was back, he was free, and would see him right away. Mr Chrimes stretched himself to his full height, took off his bowler but kept on his gloves, and firmly clenched his umbrella and plastic bag of groceries as he went through the door.

The superintendent was writing as Mr Chrimes entered, and he deliberately chose to ignore his visitor as he approached the desk. Mr Chrimes did not wait long before coughing loudly and suddenly. Matt Thornton started at the unexpected noise and looked up irritably.

'Oh, it's you, is it, Chrimes? Well, sit down.'

Mr Chrimes did as he was told and quietly gave out a long breath as he lowered himself on to the worn and wobbly chair that had been there over 30 years to his knowledge.

Matt Thornton grunted. 'I've called you in here to tell you to stop meddling in police affairs,' he said bluntly.

'And which affairs of the police am I supposed to 'ave been meddling in?' Mr Chrimes assumed an inoffensive expression which only tended to infuriate the police officer.

'You know damn well what I'm talking about,' he exclaimed. 'You've been asking questions about one or two deaths we've had about these parts recently, haven't you? No use denying it,' he continued before Mr Chrimes could say a word. 'I have it on very good authority, and it's going to stop.'

Mr Chrimes scratched the side of his nose with the umbrella handle. 'I've no intention of denying anything,' he declared. 'And I've no intention, either, of doing your job for you. If my memory serves me right, and it usually does, you dismissed any connection between these "deaths" as purely co-in-ci-dental, didn't you? All nothingness and coincidence, you said.'

'What I said has nothing to do with it.' The superintendent banged his fist angrily on the desk. 'I'm not answerable to you or to anyone else for the action I take and I will decide whether any action needs taking on any particular incident. Is that clear?'

'Yes. So you 'ave started to make enquiries about these deaths then, 'ave you. The coincidence bit is rubbing off now, is it, now there's seven of the beggars.'

'Don't you cross-examine me,' cried the superintendent, jabbing his finger in the direction of Mr Chrimes's adam's apple. 'I'm in charge here, and what I say goes. And if you insist on pursuing your own stupid, private investigations, I'll have you for obstructing the police in the course of their duty.'

'Will you now?' Mr Chrimes had always had the ability to relax under fire, and he smiled now at the superintendent's petulance. 'And I might just mention that I brought this matter to your attention two deaths ago. Donald Margerison saw you *three* deaths ago. So please don't threaten me, Mr Thornton.'

'Now look here, Chrimes. This is a very delicate matter and has to be handled with the utmost tact. Panic could well ensue if word of this got about.'

'That's why you've allocated one sergeant and one constable to it,' declared Mr Chrimes.

'Who told you that?' Matt Thornton cried. 'Come on, who've you been talking to? I'll have his scalp for this. Who was it? I'll get to know if it's the last thing I do.'

'Seven deaths,' mused Mr Chrimes. 'One sergeant, one constable...'

'How I handle this matter is my affair!' Matt Thornton's northern accent always grew stronger when he was excited, and Mr Chrimes wondered what the members of the Rotary would think now if they could hear him. 'There is no evidence yet that all these killings ... these deaths ... have been linked.'

'Crimes!' snorted Mr Chrimes. 'Don't get on that tack again. Presumably, Fred Williamson 'ad words with you about our visit to see 'im the night Billy Fleet died. Fred 'imself dies, right under your own protective eye, and you try to tell me you still don't ... per'aps you 'ave some other theory.'

'I told you. I am not discussing my actions with you. Nor my theories. I called you in here simply to tell you to stop these private investigations. And you will do well to heed my warning.'

'I'm not answerable to you, Mr Thornton. Not any longer. For some reason of your own you choose to play this affair down, and while you tactfully deal with this "delicate matter", there is a good chance of four other people, one of 'oom came to me for 'elp, losing their lives. Now I shan't get in anybody's way, but I must tell you I 'ave no intention whatsoever of stopping asking questions. By the way … did you know that Ray McCarthy 'ad been 'aving an affair with Mortimer Shelby's missus?'

'How do you know that?' the superintendent asked, scornfully.

'I've been asking questions.'

'What's it matter anyway?'

'Well, it was Shelby's car that knocked McCarthy down, wasn't it?'

'Somebody stole his car,' said the police officer.

''E could 'ave been driving it 'imself.'

'No he couldn't,' the superintendent replied quickly.

''Ow do you know that for certain?'

'Because, well … just because, that's why.'

'Just because?' said Mr Chrimes slowly, as if dealing with a child.

'I told you before, Chrimes, don't you interrogate me. Now I'm busy. Just stop these private investigations of yours, and we'll say no more about the matter. Now I must get back to my work. Good day.'

Mr Chrimes had plenty to think about as he walked home. The immediate prospect of mashed cauliflower and butter pleased him immensely, and it was a long time since he had looked forward so much to a trip as that to Scotland the following day with Donald.

His mind, too, was full of Joe Kenny and Ossie Smethurst, Mortimer Shelby and Matt Thornton, and that strange young fellow, Bebbington...

TWELVE

Mr Chrimes was soon in bed that night. He had to be up early for Donald arriving to collect him in the morning – he had said he would be there by eight o'clock, maybe even earlier – and while he was looking forward with keen anticipation to the journey, he knew the long ride by car would be tiring. And the earlier he arose in the morning, the earlier he would get into his stride. He set the alarm for six o'clock, wakened at quarter to, and had shaved and was eating his toast by quarter past.

Donald, who had been having difficulty sleeping since the deaths of Billy Fleet and Sir Fred Williamson, was also early, and arrived to find Mr Chrimes smartly attired in his grey suit and as excited as a bride on her wedding day.

'I'm all ready, Donald,' he declared. He tapped the plastic bag he had hung over the back of the chair. 'Boiled 'am sandwiches, oatmeal cakes, and a thermos containing 'ot chocolate.' He put his arm through the handles of the bag, gripped a small, brown, battered, ancient-looking attaché case with clasps but no lock, and reached for his overcoat, umbrella, bowler and gloves.

'Let me help, Mr Chrimes,' offered Donald.

'Thank you, Donald, very kind of you.'

Mr Chrimes settled himself into the passenger seat as Donald pulled out into the traffic, which was still fairly thin.

'Do you know,' said Mr Chrimes, 'that I 'ave never been any further north than Keswick and no further south than 'Eacham?'

Donald looked puzzled. 'Where's that?'

'Near 'Unstanton. On the Wash, you know. I've never been one for travelling. Morecambe and St Annes were far enough for our 'olidays, Mrs Chrimes and me, and I always looked on Scotland as I would going abroad to France or Belgium or somewhere. Yet I always wanted to go. Silly, isn't it?'

Donald made good time to Fort William and then took the main road towards Inverness. 'Our place is only small, but I'm sure it will be signposted,' said Donald. 'So if you'll keep an eye open, Mr Chrimes, for Inverneilen. We can only be a few miles away.'

The two of them peered through the

windscreen at every sign, and only a few minutes later, Mr Chrimes shouted. 'Did you see that, did you see that?'

'Yes, Loch-something or other, wasn't it?'

'Lochtamman!' exclaimed Mr Chrimes. 'Lochtamman!'

'Should I have heard of it?' asked Donald.

'Indeed you should. That's where Sir Fred Williamson was when 'e was shot through the 'ead!'

From the sign off to Lochtamman, it was less than seven miles to the village of Inverneilen. Luke Smiddy, so Mr Chrimes had been led to believe, lived in a large house near the village, and it was the two travellers' intention to seek out their fellow Old Skelhamian the following morning.

The only inn, which stood next to the only church, could not accommodate visitors, and they were re-directed to a farm 800 yards further along where Morag McTavish was only too welcome to oblige them. She showed them to their rooms, clean, white-washed rooms with solid oak furniture and comfortable beds. After apologising for being caught unawares and not having sufficient food in the house for guests, she fed them on sausages, eggs, ham and chips.

She heaped brown bread and white bread

and butter on them, scones and jam, home-made cakes, and large cups of tea. Only when they had finished and made themselves comfortable in front of a roaring log fire did Mrs McTavish, a widow, ask her visitors where they were from.

The journey, the meal, and the fire had all combined to make Mr Chrimes feel drowsy, and for once it was Donald who conducted the conversation. He told her they were from Skelham, a place she had never heard of, that he worked for a building society, that Mr Chrimes, who was rapidly dozing off, was retired but had been a policeman, and was making his first visit to Scotland.

'And what are you doing in these parts?' Mrs McTavish had few visitors and she enjoyed company, even if one of them did drop off to sleep in front of her roaring fire.

'We're going to see Luke Smiddy,' explained Donald. 'We all went to the same school. Do you know him, by any chance?'

'Oh yes, everybody knows him around these parts.'

'Do you see much of him?'

'Well, he hasn't been too well recently,' said Mrs McTavish as she drew a stool up to the fire and sat between the two men. 'In fact, Mrs Dalgaird was telling me only this very day that she had heard from Archie – he's the milkman, ye ken – that he's seriously ill. Now I don't know how much truth there is in it,' she added hastily. 'But I know we haven't seen him around for a week or two. Why he lives in that great, rambling house, I just do not know.'

The references to Luke Smiddy had drawn Mr Chrimes from his slumber, and he eased himself up in his chair.

'Is 'e living on 'is own?' he asked.

'Well, he's got the man who looks after him, that's all. What do you call them? Not a valet, nothing like that. More a companion. Or secretary.'

'And 'e's been ill, you say?'

'Yes. Somebody did say it was cancer.'

'So 'e won't 'ave been out this week at all?'

'Well, I haven't seen him. Mind you, he's been up and down with his illness. People said he was dying not so long ago, thought he wasn't long for this world, then up he gets and off. Strong old man he is.'

'Do you like him?' Donald asked.

'I couldn't say I dislike him. Not the sort of man, I wouldn't say, that you could hate. But then again…'

'Not the sort you could take to, either,' put in Mr Chrimes. ''E was always like that.

Maybe it was the money.'

'He's certainly made a lot of that,' said Mrs McTavish. 'And where will it all go to when he's gone, that's the question? Mr Grampain – he's the butcher, ye ken – he said he'd heard that apart from some bequest to his manservant, it's all going to charity, mainly Cancer Research.'

'But I thought 'e 'ad a sister. Oh, but she was older than 'im anyway, so I suppose she might 'ave popped off.'

'Sam Mocton did say she had a son, didn't he?' declared Donald.

'That's right, 'e did. But if she was older than Luke, and we don't know 'ow much older, 'e could 'ave passed on as well.'

'That reminds me,' said Mrs McTavish. 'Last summer, I think it was, a man, an Englishman, was up here to see Mr Smiddy. I do believe Mrs Campbell – she runs the Post Office, ye ken – said it was a nephew. At least, I think she did.'

'All to charity,' mused Mr Chrimes. 'There's worse places it could go to, I suppose. There'll be a lot of money, and if it 'elps to save lives, it'll 'ave been of use.'

'And there is a lot,' said Mrs McTavish. 'I did hear – now who was it told me? I'm getting very forgetful these days, ye ken –

that it would be over a million. Now I think if I had that sort of money, I'd have a few guards or an Alsatian or two round that house. People have been murdered in their beds for much less than that!'

Mr Chrimes and Donald slept soundly – and safely – that night. Their beds were clean and comfortable and warmed by the hot-water bottles Mrs McTavish put in after they arrived. Mr Chrimes fell asleep soon after his head touched the pillow, rocked for a few moments by the continuing movement of the car. Donald, however, stayed awake for a time. He drew back his curtains and stared out into the blackest night he had ever seen. They say the sky was like that during the war, he thought. But he was too young to remember. The almost utter silence was new to him, too, and he had to strain his ears to pick up the occasional sound, like the hooting of a distant owl, or the clink of empty milk bottles being put out.

As he stared and listened, he thought about the men who had died, and the man who might have been responsible for their deaths, Luke Smiddy. Could they be near the end of the trail? Would Mr Chrimes be able to bring to an end tomorrow the spate of killings that had taken almost an entire cricket team? Mr Chrimes's words came back to him as his eye-lids drooped, and sleep overtook him: 'Just think yourself lucky you were a bowler, Donald, 'oo batted so badly you went in last...'

A crisp morning greeted the two men. The feebleness of the sun had had little effect on the frost, and Donald shivered at the sight of the cold, white ground. As he opened the window to look out, the faint sound of bag-pipes floated up to him, coming, it seemed, from the direction of the village.

'Ay, that will be Flora Straithes,' explained Mrs McTavish as she set two large helpings of porridge in front of her guests. 'This is the only time she gets to practise.'

'A woman ... playing the bagpipes!' exclaimed Donald.

'And why not?' said Mrs McTavish. 'We women are just as emaciated up here as you are in England.'

Mr Chrimes spluttered over his porridge, which was followed by fresh, warm rolls with butter and a choice of marmalade, apricot or damson jam. Each sank two cups of tea, and while the morning was still as fresh and as welcome as the rolls, they followed Mrs McTavish's directions to Luke Smiddy's house.

The house, stone-built, was vast. It could not be seen from the entrance which stood at the end of a badly-rutted lane down which Donald had driven his car with the utmost care. The gates to the drive were open and as Donald hesitated, wondering whether to leave the car at the entrance, Mr Chrimes boomed: 'ON, Donald, ON. Straight on!' The drive turned sharply to the right after 40 yards to reveal the splendid Victorian mansion, set on a rise but shielded from the lane and the village by a plantation of firs. Another car stood near the entrance and Donald pulled up alongside it. Mr Chrimes knocked on the elegant, oak door in his usual challenging fashion and was soon confronted by a tall, well-built, heavily bearded man who Mr Chrimes took to be in his fifties. His hair, too, was long, his eyebrows were bushy, and there was precious little skin on the man's head or face which was exposed to the air. Yet there was something about the face which looked familiar to Mr Chrimes and which set his brain working frantically.

'Good morning!' bellowed Mr Chrimes. 'We've come to see Mr Smiddy.'

'I'm sorry,' replied the man. 'Mr Smiddy is ill and the doctor is with him at the moment.'

'But we've come three 'undred miles to see 'im,' exclaimed Mr Chrimes.

'I'm sorry, but like I say...' The man started to shut the door, but Mr Chrimes quickly stuck his size eleven boot over the step to stop it.

'Now look here,' the man began. 'I have told you Mr Smiddy's ill and unable to...'

'What is it, James?' The strong Scottish voice came from inside and was soon followed by an elderly, bustling man with a stethoscope in one hand and a black, doctor's bag in the other.

'These men have come to see the master, doctor. I told them he was too ill to see anybody.'

'Doctor, we've come three 'undred miles to see Luke,' Mr Chrimes declared forcibly. 'And it is important.'

The doctor looked down at Mr Chrimes's foot, and then said: 'Well, James, when people have come three hundred miles I think we can at least afford them some hospitality and bid them enter, eh?'

James pouted sulkily as he slowly opened the door to allow the visitors to enter the stone-flagged hall, largely covered by a beautifully-designed Oriental carpet.

'Now, gentleman,' said the doctor as

James closed the door behind them. 'What was it ye wanted?'

Mr Chrimes introduced himself – 'recently retired police officer, doctor' – and Donald, explained his past connection with Luke Smiddy, and then added: 'It is important we see 'im, but I'm sorry, I cannot divulge the reason for our visit. Is it possible to see 'im for a little while?'

The doctor stuffed the stethoscope into the bag. 'Normally I'd say not. He's had a bad night and needs rest. But ye have come a long way, ye're old friends, and seeing it is important ... I'll go and have a word with him. I'll not keep ye a minute.'

He took the stairs two at a time like a sprightly medical student, leaving Mr Chrimes and Donald in the hall. James moved forward: 'Can I take your coat, sir?'

'No thank you, we'll not be 'ere long.' Mr Chrimes could not trace the English part of James's cosmopolitan accent which developed Scottish tendencies only occasionally. ''Aven't we met before somewhere?' he asked.

The brown eyes, heavily hooded by hair, blinked rapidly. 'Not that I recall, sir.'

''Ave you ever been to Skelham or thereabouts?'

189

'Well sir, Mr Smiddy has been to those parts on occasions, and I have usually accompanied him.'

'I've seen you somewhere. Sure I 'ave. It'll come back to me.'

The conversation was interrupted by the doctor, who leaned over the stairs to shout: 'This way gentlemen, if you please.'

Mr Chrimes and Donald made their way up the winding staircase to join the doctor, who whispered to them: 'Don't mind James. He means well, but he's inclined to be just a wee bit over-protective. Ye'll find Luke is rather tired and quite weak, so I can allow ye only a few minutes. If ye could be as brief as possible?' He smiled at them, and opened the door into a large, tastefully-furnished bedroom, in which a huge fire was burning. The doctor walked over to the bed where Luke Smiddy lay, the bedclothes up to his neck, his head slightly raised as it rested on three pillows. 'Luke, there are the visitors I was telling ye about. I've told them only a few minutes.' The doctor smiled on the visitors again, then left the room.

Luke Smiddy looked stronger than Mr Chrimes expected. His eyes were clear and alert, and he had clearly been shaved that morning. Mr Chrimes made his way to the bedside and a hand slipped out from under the covers and gripped his.

'Joseph Chrimes! Well I'm blessed.' Luke Smiddy cackled throatily and his eyes smiled warmly. 'How long has it been?'

Mr Chrimes sat on a chair near the head of the bed, a chair still warm from its previous occupant, the doctor. 'Twenty-five years I suppose, Luke. Must be twenty-five.'

'And who's this with you?'

Donald stepped forward. 'Margerison, Mr Smiddy. Donald Margerison.'

Luke Smiddy's eyes turned cold. 'Oh yes, I know you as well, don't I? D. J. Margerison, opening bowler. Am I right?'

Donald was flustered. 'Ye-e-e-s,' he stammered.

'And number eleven batsman!'

''Ow the 'ell 'ave you remembered that, Luke?' asked Mr Chrimes in amazement. 'All those years and you trot it out like it was yesterday.'

'Let's see,' Smiddy croaked. 'D. J. Margerison l.b.w. Shelby for nought, wasn't it? Took two wickets as well.'

'Fantastic!' exclaimed Mr Chrimes.

'Don't fanny me, Joseph. Not a match I'm ever likely to forget, is it? I thought of taking that scorecard to the grave with me. I know it better than I've ever known anything in my life. When I was at school and we used to have to learn all those poems and things off by heart, I couldn't remember one. Two lines and I ground to a halt. That was a failing that's been with me all my life. Yet that match is imprinted on my brain as if a man with a rubber stamp had hammered every name, every score, every detail on it.'

He had lifted his head from the pillow as he spat out the words. He let it fall back and began to breathe quickly as he looked at the ceiling.

'But why did you 'arbour it, Luke. Why? 'Asn't time 'ealed the wounds of that match at all?'

Luke Smiddy brought his eyes down to meet Mr Chrimes's. 'I had always believed in cricket, Joseph. And all it stood for. It was a game for gentlemen, for sportsmen. Whatever happened in business – and that could be dirty at times – I always returned to cricket for its cleanness, its honesty. The game helped me maintain some values, I suppose.'

'But one game, Luke,' pleaded Mr Chrimes. 'Surely you didn't see those values collapse because of one incident in one game?'

'The game was like business, Joseph. The players were overcome with greed. They were so greedy to win, they would cheat to achieve their ends. I can still remember several faces in that school team when I told them I hadn't touched the ball. They leered. They wanted rid of me, and it didn't matter how. And if that wasn't enough, somebody made a mess of my car. It wasn't just being out when I knew I could have won the match on my own. An ideal had been destroyed, by my own school, and I hated them for it.'

'All of them?'

'Oh yes. In a team game even the most insignificant member plays his part in victory or defeat. And every man is a party to team behaviour. You step forward when you see wrong being done, but nobody stepped forward that day. Nobody tried to stop me being given out, nobody apologised. NOBODY!'

Again, Luke Smiddy sank back on the pillows, exhausted. Mr Chrimes looked at Donald, then back again to the sick man, who was having difficulty breathing.

'Anyway, what have you come here for?' Smiddy gasped. He looked from one man to the other. 'It's to do with that match, isn't it? You want to stop me...'

He flopped on to the pillows yet again and the harsh, rasping noise from his throat alarmed Mr Chrimes who jumped to his feet. 'I'll get the doctor,' he declared.

Luke Smiddy held up his hand. 'Don't bother,' he panted. 'There's nothing he can do. I'll decide if I live or die.'

Mr Chrimes sat down quickly and leaned forward. 'Luke! You're right. It 'as to stop,' he said softly. 'Too many lives 'ave been lost already because of that one mistake, that one terrible mistake.'

Smiddy stared deep into Mr Chrimes' eyes. Then, to the surprise of his two visitors, he started to cackle again, his body rocking on the bed as he found the energy to laugh. When he had finished, he turned to Donald and asked: 'And what's the count at the moment, D. J. Margerison?'

'SEVEN!' Donald blurted it out and was surprised how loud it sounded to him. 'Seven killed,' he repeated.

'Seven?' exclaimed Smiddy croakily. 'That *is* a lot. The Magnificent Seven! And which seven would they be, D. J. Margerison,' he demanded like a schoolmaster.

'THE FIRST SEVEN!' Donald shouted.

'Seven wickets down!' Luke Smiddy looked to have regained some of his energy and he

194

started to snigger. 'Well, I'm blessed.'

'Why, Luke?' Mr Chrimes appealed to him. 'Why?'

'I thought you'd come here because you knew why, Joseph. But you don't, do you. You don't.'

'Not revenge Luke. Not revenge for being cheated out in a cricket match. I can't believe that.'

'What can you believe, Joseph?' Smiddy cackled again. 'Well, I'm blessed. I wouldn't have believed it… And you want me to tell you why.'

The extra energy he had expounded suddenly took its toll. His breathing became heavily laboured and the blood drained from his face as he gasped for air.

'The doctor, Donald. Quick!' ordered Mr Chrimes.

Donald leapt from his chair and dashed for the door. Mr Chrimes, knowing he might never have another opportunity to ask Luke Smiddy anything, leaned forward till his mouth was an inch away from the sick man's ear.

'Why, Luke? Just tell me why.'

Smiddy tried desperately to take in great gulps of air, biting viciously at the emptiness.

'Why, Luke?' Mr Chrimes hissed.

Their eyes met. 'Ask...' croaked Luke Smiddy in a voice that was barely audible.

Mr Chrimes heard the sound of feet running up the stairs. Another few seconds and he wouldn't get another word out of him.

'Ask 'oo?' he demanded.

Luke Smiddy bit at the air again and again. 'You ask Matt,' he gasped. 'He knows all about it.'

The door burst open and the doctor dashed in, quickly followed by Donald. He bent his head to listen to his patient's heart, then looked to his eyes. 'Take it easy,' he said soothingly. 'Soon be all right. Ye need rest.' He turned away from the bed. 'I'll have to ask ye to leave now, gentlemen. He's exhausted. I'm sorry, but ye can see, he isn't fit to talk any more. It must all have been too much for him.'

The two men returned to the hall and waited there for the doctor to join them.

''Ow long 'as 'e been like that, doctor?' Mr Chrimes asked.

'Just a couple of days. He was right as rain earlier in the week. He was badly like this three or four weeks ago, and how he pulled through I don't know. Will-power, I suppose.'

'So 'e was well enough earlier in the week to 'ave gone out.'

'Oh yes. He frequently trots off on little excursions. Some rather big ones as well. James will tell ye better than me. That's so James, isn't it? Wasn't the master out before he began to feel unwell on Friday?'

James stayed by his post at the front door. 'You know as well as me, doctor, the master never liked being cooped up in here. Liked to get out when he could.'

'And 'e's been out this week, 'as 'e?' said Mr Chrimes.

'Well ... yes, of course,' James replied, hesitantly. 'But there's nothing unusual in that.'

'Now did I say there was? Where did you go?'

'Me? Where did I go?'

'Well, I assume you drive your master around.'

'Not everywhere. Some places he likes to drive himself. Go on his own.'

'And 'e did that this week?'

'Yes, he did. I don't know where he went. If he doesn't say, I don't ask. Not my place to.'

'Did 'e stay overnight?'

'Not he. Doesn't like spending his nights

away from here more than he needs. Might spend the whole day away, early morning till late at night, but he does like his own bed, does the master.'

'So you 'aven't taken 'im anywhere this week?'

'Not exactly,' James replied.

'Oh! Well, where did you go?'

James hesitated before replying. 'The master was invited out on Thursday,' he stuttered. 'Just up the road, but there was an unfortunate occurrence soon after we got there, so the master left immediately. Straight back here we came.'

'And what unfortunate occurrence was this?' demanded Mr Chrimes.

'Some chap blew his brains out with a gun!'

'Ask Matt, 'e said. Matt knows all about it.' Mr Chrimes had sat quietly for several minutes after he and Donald had left the house and set off on the long journey home. Then he started to think aloud. 'Ask Matt. 'E knows all about it.'

'Matt Thornton is that, Mr Chrimes?'

''E's the only Matt I know that Luke Smiddy can know as well,' declared Mr Chrimes. 'And Matt Thornton fits rather well into this puzzle, so I daresay it was 'im 'e meant. But if that's so, what is it that Superintendent Thornton knows that's so vital to this matter, something 'e's keeping well and truly to 'imself?'

'Something about the match that we haven't heard about?' ventured Donald.

'Could be. Something that was per'aps drawn to the attention of the police that Matt Thornton knew about then, or 'as since learned in 'is 'igher capacity as a Super-Duper.'

'Do you think maybe Joe Kenny's vandalising of Mr Smiddy's car was reported to the police, and there were some repercussions we don't know about?'

'Re-per-cussions,' repeated Mr Chrimes slowly as he stared through the windscreen, his eyes glazed and noticing nothing as he concentrated on the conversation he had just held with Luke Smiddy.

'Do you think Luke Smiddy could have committed all the killings then, Mr Chrimes?'

Mr Chrimes stopped staring through the windscreen and turned his attention to Donald. 'Judged on what we 'ave just witnessed, Donald, I would say yes, 'e could 'ave. 'E's still uncommonly bitter towards the players in that match – look at the way 'e greeted you. Downright nasty it was, especially seeing as 'ow you'd come three 'undred miles just to see 'im as well.'

'And he did ask if you had come to stop him,' suggested Donald, eagerly.

'Yes, that's true, Donald, that's very true. But did 'e look strong enough to you to drive all of six 'undred miles only last week to kill Billy Fleet and then be responsible for the death of Fred Williamson as well?'

'But they did say he was up and down with his illness,' pointed out Donald, who desperately wanted the dying Luke Smiddy to have been responsible for the seven deaths. 'And didn't he say so himself?'

'That's true, Donald.' Mr Chrimes nodded his head sagely. 'That's very true.'

'He didn't say you didn't know who had done the killings, did he? He said you didn't know why. And perhaps Matt Thornton will be able to assist there.'

'What about that manservant of 'is? James … James … James what I wonder. I rarely forget a face and 'is nearly came back to me once in the 'ouse. Where 'ave I seen 'im before. Where?'

Mr Chrimes went quiet after this and resumed his thoughtful staring out of the window. Donald, too, left the subject alone as he concentrated on his route home.

It was as they were approaching Glencoe that Mr Chrimes suddenly sprang back into life, slapping his knee hard as he exclaimed: 'Got it! That's 'oo 'e is!'

'Who who is?' said Donald.

''Oo 'oo is?' repeated Mr Chrimes playfully. 'You sound like a demented owl, Donald. 'Oo James is, of course. I knew I'd seen 'im before. Never forget a face.' He was clearly pleased with himself, but Donald was becoming infuriated at not being told who Luke Smiddy's manservant really was.

'It was the James bit that threw me,' explained Mr Chrimes. 'Shouldn't 'ave thought about that at all.'

'That's not his real name then?' demanded Donald.

'Oh yes. Yes it is.'

Donald looked puzzled. 'Then why did it throw you?'

'Because it's 'is second Christian name. Terence James Gilmichael 'e's called. Always used to be Terence or Terry. Never used the James bit.'

'And where do you know him from?'

'Now that's the question, isn't it? Faces and names I can put together. Where from isn't always so easy. There was a case several years ago – 'Eavens, it must be twenty years ago or more – involving three or four people. And if my memory serves me right, it was something serious like assault. It wasn't my case really, as I recall. Now was I brought in part way through, or did I 'ave to go to court with it. Or what? Anyway, no matter. I'll be down at the station tomorrow, and Sandy will fill in the details for me.'

'Sandy?' enquired Donald.

'Friend of mine in records,' explained Mr Chrimes. 'I still 'ave quite a few friends down there.'

THIRTEEN

Mr Chrimes was late rising the following morning. All the travelling and excitement of the previous two days had left him weary, and he was in no hurry to get out of his bed. By the time he left the house it was almost noon and he decided to collect some groceries from Ossie and Joe's before going to the station. Smethurst and Kenny's, Grocers, however, was closed. The blinds were drawn, but there wasn't a notice to say why the shop was not open as usual. Mr Chrimes bustled round to the back of the shop, and opened the gate to a stack of crates of milk, delivered earlier from the dairy. His first reaction was one of alarm. Then he recalled Joe asking if they should go away if their lives were in danger. Ossie had stoutly resisted the suggestion, but he could have had second thoughts. If they had gone away, however, wouldn't they have done what any careful citizen would do – stop the milk! Mr Chrimes thought about it on the way to the station, and thought the most probable solution was that Ossie and Joe had decided to take a sudden holiday. In any case, he would mention it to Matt Thornton. Better look willing, he thought.

He had a word with his friend in records, Sandy, before going to the superintendent's office. Yes, Superintendent Thornton would see him, but could he wait a minute. The minute turned into ten, the ten into half an hour before the superintendent was ready to see him.

'What is it you want?' asked the police officer brusquely as Mr Chrimes walked in. The desk was awash with paper and Mr Chrimes decided there had either been a Criminals' Convention in Skelham over the weekend, or Superintendent Thornton was trying to impress.

This, again, was no time for preamble, so Mr Chrimes sat down and said firmly: 'I saw Luke Smiddy yesterday. 'E mentioned you.'

The superintendent, who had been writing frantically, stopped immediately. He did not look up for a few seconds, then slowly raised his head just far enough so he could look at Mr Chrimes.

'I warned you, didn't I, about interfering,' he said slowly. 'I told you to keep your nose out of police affairs and NOT, repeat NOT, go meddling.'

'Me? Meddling? 'Eaven forbid. Bless you, Superintendent, I was doing no more than call on an old friend, a fellow Old Boy of Skelham Grammar School, asking about 'is welfare.'

'Don't give me that, Chrimes. You asked him about that stupid match when he was cheated on, didn't you?'

'Well, one thing did lead to another and as a matter of fact, yes, that was among the topics raised.'

'Now don't you mess about with me, Chrimes,' barked the superintendent. 'Or you'll find you've picked the wrong man. Now what were you doing in Scotland, seeing Luke Smiddy?'

'Just paying a friendly visit, a very friendly visit. 'E's not well, you know. They do say 'e's dying. Did you know that?'

'No, I did not. I have enough of my own problems without bothering over somebody I haven't seen for donkey's years. Apart from those cricket matches I knew very little about the man.'

'Is that so?' Mr Chrimes asked. 'That's not what 'e said about you!'

The superintendent narrowed his eyes and glowered at Mr Chrimes. 'And what the bloody hell were you doing discussing me with Luke Smiddy?' he snarled.

'We weren't exactly discussing you,' Mr Chrimes explained patiently. 'I just 'appened to mention all these 'ere deaths there'd been…'

'Just as I thought,' the superintendent snapped.

'…when your name cropped up.'

'And tell me, how did my name just happen to crop up?'

'Luke Smiddy suggested that *you* would be able to throw some light on the matter. In fact, if I understand 'im right, you'd do more than that, you'd explain the 'ole matter, lock, stock and barrel.'

'Me?' thundered Superintendent Thornton. 'ME? He probably knows I think it's a load of stuff and nonsense.'

'And 'ow would 'e be after knowing that?'

'Don't ask me.' The superintendent leaned back in his chair and swivelled slightly away from his visitor.

''E said you'd know why there'd been all these killings.'

'Oh don't start that rubbish again, it's no…'

'Did you know Luke Smiddy was also at Lochtamman the day Fred Williamson died?'

The superintendent looked startled. 'No, I didn't. He told you that, did he?'

'No. As a matter of fact, it was 'is man-servant. A chap we've 'ad on our books down 'ere, name of Terence James Gilmichael. Done for assault, I think it was.'

'Never heard of him,' said Matt Thornton without hesitation. 'There have been rather a lot of undesirables through my hands through the years, you know.'

'Seems 'e drove Luke Smiddy to Lochtamman, and they left as soon as they got there and 'eard about the shooting. So 'e said.'

'And you think Luke Smiddy might have been responsible,' the police officer sneered.

'I don't know what to think,' Mr Chrimes replied. 'I did 'ope you'd be able to 'elp. Luke said you would.'

'Well, Luke's wrong.'

'Did you know it was Joe Kenny 'oo wrecked Luke's car after that infamous match of ours?'

Superintendent Thornton stared in disbelief at Mr Chrimes. 'How did you know that?' he cried.

'A little bird told me.'

'Don't you be clever with me, Chrimes, or you'll find yourself up for...'

'Up for nothing, Mr Thornton. You're forgetting again. I'm a common citizen now. Yes, Joe Kenny it was. 'Im as wouldn't 'urt a fly. A few people knew about it. Didn't you?'

'I told you before and I'm telling you again. Don't you interrogate me, Chrimes. You're no longer a member of the force, as you're so fond of telling me, and what I do, what I know, is my business.'

'Another thing,' persisted Mr Chrimes in his strident voice. 'Did you know that Ossie and Joe 'aven't opened their shop today?'

'What's the matter?' scoffed the superintendent. 'Is the cheese starting to smell? You have been a proper little detective, haven't you?'

'Well somebody 'as to be.' Mr Chrimes said the words slowly. He was perfectly relaxed and stared Matt Thornton in the eye. 'And before you ask what it 'as to do with you, do you remember they are next in the batting order.'

'Ossie Smethurst and Joe Kenny will do as they wish with their business. I strongly advise you, Chrimes, to mind yours. Now. I'm very busy...'

The shop was still closed when Mr Chrimes retraced his steps through the Market Square, so he turned in the direction of their home on the old Bayfield Road, swinging his arms energetically as he went. There was no reply, either at the front or back, to his knocking, so he left for home, determined to make sure something would be done the following day if the two men had still not appeared.

Amy Charles enjoyed being a char. She did for Alderman and Mrs Henry Bagslate on Mondays, Wednesdays and Fridays, and for Ossie and Joe on Tuesdays, Thursdays and Saturday mornings. Of the two, she preferred going to Ossie and Joe's. Mrs Bagslate was too fussy by half, always standing over her, finding bits of dusting she'd missed, squeezing every last minute's work out of her, and making sure she didn't have so much as a smell of the whisky. Even on cold mornings like these.

Ossie and Joe were different. To start with, they weren't there when she did for them. They were at the shop. So she had the place to herself, and while she might take the odd liberty here and there – 'Well, you need something to keep the cold out, don't you, love' – she did them a proper job. And there'd never been any complaints. Never. Some people looked down their noses at

Ossie and Joe living together like man and wife, but Amy Charles prided herself on her broadmindedness. They'd never done her any harm, paid her on the dot, and what they did was their own business. Amy was a woman of the world. There wasn't much that would shock her.

The sight of a dead body, however, was enough to give her the screaming convulsions, and when she found Ossie Smethurst on that Tuesday morning, his throat cut from ear to ear – 'and in his own kitchen, too' – they said her screeching could be heard as far away as the Town Hall.

Donald heard about Ossie's death at lunchtime, and he was ready when the distinctive hammering came at his front door soon after he got home that evening.

''Ave you 'eard?'

Donald said yes he had, and he had intended calling on Mr Chrimes as soon as he had had his tea, and what did it all mean now that Luke Smiddy was seriously ill in his bed in the Scottish Highlands.

But 'ad 'e 'eard the rest?

'Before I tell you about Ossie, Donald, a bit of choice information about one Terence James Gilmichael, Luke Smiddy's man-servant-cum-secretary-cum-dogsbody. You may recall I said I thought 'e 'ad been up for assault or some such offence. 'Ow I forgot I don't know, but it was grevious bodily assault on a police constable *after* 'e 'ad been arrested for causing considerable damage to a shop in the market square. And 'oose shop was it? 'Oose shop did this 'ere servant of Luke Smiddy's tear to pieces? Why, none other than ... Ossie and Joe's!'

Mr Chrimes paused after this piece of shattering information, timing his pause with the precision of an actor before continuing: 'It was a weekend, and this 'ere James broke into the shop late at night. You've never seen such a mess, like a whirlwind 'ad 'it it. For good measure 'e decides to break the plate-glass window, which brings the aforesaid, unfortunate constable onto the scene. 'E managed to get James back to the station peaceful enough, but then all 'ell breaks loose again and the constable's uniform is torn, 'e breaks a finger, and is off duty for I don't know 'ow long. At the time, it was all put down to drink. There wasn't any apparent motive and James got off rather lightly.'

'And was he Luke Smiddy's manservant *then?*'

'It seem so. 'E gave 'is occupation as manservant, and 'is address was in Inverneilen.'

'So he could have been acting on orders?'

'Precisely. A devoted "manservant" is James, 'oo might very well benefit rather 'andsomely when Luke dies and leaves 'is fortune. That's interesting bit of news, number one, Donald. Now for number two. Ossie Smethurst, as you might 'ave 'eard, 'ad 'is throat cut by 'is own bread knife. And the only prints on that bread knife? Why, 'is own and Joe's naturally enough. But where's Joe, you might say? Vamoosed. Scarpered. There's a rather flashy suitcase gone – the woman 'oo does for them soon noticed that and with it rather a lot of Joe's clothes. The car is missing, too, and a full-scale 'unt was launched late this afternoon to find Joe Kenny, "wanted by the police to 'elp them in their enquiries." Now what do you think about that?'

'I don't know what to say,' replied Donald, who looked stunned. 'One minute it's Luke Smiddy, perhaps with the help of his manservant, the next it's Joe Kenny the police are after. Well, at least it's really got Matt Thornton moving now.'

'Oh yes,' agreed Mr Chrimes. "'E's got 'is teeth into this one good and proper.'

Joe Kenny's face was pictured in every news-paper the following morning, and Skelham buzzed with gossip about two of the town's best-known inhabitants. He was found within two days, only six miles from his home, dead from exposure on the moors. He was lying in a trench, dressed in a smart, brown, mohair suit he had had specially made only three weeks earlier. The temper-ature had dropped to freezing point over the last two or three nights and Superintendent Thornton quickly decided that after killing his lifelong friend Ossie, Joe, in his panic, had decided to go in hiding on the moors, and been frozen to death. But no reason was given for his having abandoned the car three miles away, and it was seen fit to ignore the rope marks around both wrists.

The discovery of Joe's body filled Donald with a new and even deeper fear, and as soon as he had finished work on the Thurs-day, he drove round to Mr Chrimes's home. Mr Chrimes was making his tea, and as he dropped three rashers of streaky bacon into his frying pan, he listened to Donald unload his feelings.

'I'm frightened, Mr Chrimes!' he declared. 'To be honest, I'm scared to death. There's only Bebbington and me, and if they are going in twos now, I could be struck down at any minute. Joe Kenny solves all Matt Thornton's problems, I suppose, but I know it only means I'm next-but-one on the list.' His voice started to rise as he filled himself with alarm. 'There's no telling when it will come, maybe even tonight, or where from! I can't...'

'Steady on Donald, steady on lad,' Mr Chrimes soothed as he pressed the bacon fat with a fork. 'I've been thinking about this. You need protection, Donald, and I think you'll be better off tonight if I come and stay with you. Get the wife off to 'er mother's again and then rest in peace tonight.'

'That's very kind of you, Mr Chrimes, but what about tomorrow, and the day after that, and the day...'

'Yes, yes, I realise all that. I've decided, Donald, to go back up to Inverneilen on Saturday, and see Luke Smiddy again. The answer's there, I'm sure it is, and I'm going to find it.'

'But how will you get there?' Donald demanded. 'I've promised to take Roseanne to the autumn fair on Saturday, I can't disappoint her.'

'I don't expect you to, Donald. There's an overnight train to Inverness and one back later in the morning. Inverneilen is only six miles from Inverness, so I'll 'ave three hours to get there and back. Plenty of time.'

'But what about me?' cried Donald. 'I'll be left on my own. I know it's only the one night, but it could happen then, couldn't it? After all, whoever is committing all these murders knows exactly what everybody is doing, doesn't he? And I can't ask Roseanne to stay with me, that wouldn't be fair. I'll ask her, see if it's all right if I come with you again. She won't mind, I'm sure.'

'There's no need, Donald,' said Mr Chrimes. He took the bacon out of the pan and put it on his plate with two slices of bread and butter. 'There's somebody, you know, 'oo is in more immediate danger then you. This lad Bebbington. Now I propose we see 'im tonight and persuade 'im to come back 'ere with the two of us, and we'll all stay together tonight. 'E'll be with you tomorrow, then I'll be back. With the answer, I 'ope!'

'Do you think he'll agree to that?' enquired Donald.

'I don't know,' Mr Chrimes replied. 'I suppose it will all depend on 'ow seriously 'e takes us. 'E could just laugh in our faces, I suppose.'

Bebbington, however, did not laugh at them. He could see that Mr Chrimes was in deadly earnest, and one look at Donald's pinched, white face was enough to convince him that death could well be just around the corner. Roseanne reluctantly allowed Donald to drive her to her mother's, on the other side of town, and by the middle of the evening the three men were sitting together in Donald's living room, discussing the situation.

'While I'm away tomorrow,' Mr Chrimes explained, 'sleep in the same bedroom. I suggest you both go to the autumn fair so you can stick together the 'ole time. It's no good saying there's no danger, but it will be reduced if you take every precaution and stay together as much as possible. You've only one night to get through, tomorrow, then I'll be back on Saturday night. And by then it's to be 'oped I'll 'ave found the answer.'

Mr Chrimes booked a sleeper for the journey, and boarded the train soon after midnight. It was the first time he had slept in a bed on a train and he was surprised how quickly he managed to get off to sleep. He awakened, refreshed, and enjoyed his tea and biscuits in bed before shaving and preparing himself to leave the train as soon as it arrived in Inverness. He toyed with the idea of a taxi to Inverneilen, but discarded the idea when he found that the buses, which ran every half-hour, passed by the station.

Inverneilen was barely stirring when Mr Chrimes arrived shortly after nine o'clock and he passed only one elderly couple in the main street as he strode briskly along it in the direction of the lane leading to Luke Smiddy's house. There were no signs of activity when he arrived, and when repeated knocking produced no reply at the front door, he made his way round the side, looking for a way into the house. He soon found a ground-floor window that had been left open and as he released it from its catch and pushed it open to its full width, Mr Chrimes knew, for the first time in his life, what it felt like to be a criminal. The curtains had been drawn at the window, heavy velvet curtains, and he had to push hard to get the window open. He looked round furtively before he pushed one leg over the sill, which he sat astride for a moment as he listened for any sounds from the house. There was none. He pulled the other leg over, parted the curtains, and entered the room.

The darkness was total. He did not want to draw back the curtains for fear of attracting attention, so he started to make his way slowly and cautiously across the room. He soon bumped against what was obviously a table and, feeling the edge, he started to make his way round it. He ran his fingers along it as he moved, stopping abruptly as he touched what felt to be a wooden box overhanging the rim of the table. He moved his hand up the smooth wood till he came to the top, his curiosity forcing his fingers to creep inside. They touched cloth that felt like silk. Then he froze. Never before had he wanted to scream, and he couldn't utter a sound. He felt his hair rise and his heart stop beating for a second as his hand touched … a human face! It seemed an hour before Mr Chrimes could force his legs to move and as quickly as he dared, he felt his way round the box, bumping into a chair before he touched the door. He soon found the light switch at the side, and ignoring the risk he was taking, turned it on. The box was a coffin! The body inside … that of Luke Smiddy.

The room was clearly the study. Just the room he would expect to hold the private documents that would help him. But he could have chosen more convivial company! He carefully opened the door and looked round the hall and up the winding staircase. No sign of life. Again he listened, but no sounds. He closed the door and as he turned, saw, on the other side of the coffin and alongside the window, a desk.

He tip-toed his way to it as if afraid of wakening the dead and as he started to search the top drawer, he was filled with an overwhelming feeling that he was being watched. The papers all concerned business and as Mr Chrimes moved down to the second drawer he glanced quickly across at the coffin to make sure Luke wasn't watching. He felt completely uncomfortable. He began to feel cold and clammy as if he were catching flu and a prickly sensation worked its way down his body.

The drawers yielded nothing of interest, and he turned his attention to the desk itself. It was locked. There had been a key at the back of the bottom drawer, and Mr Chrimes quickly found it again and inserted it in the lock. It worked, and the lid of the desk let down smoothly to reveal a mass of documents, neatly bundled or pigeon-holed. Quickly, Mr Chrimes flicked through them.

Bills of sale, bank statements, insurance documents, receipts by the score dating back 20 and 30 years, income tax forms, where was he to start? He sat down and looked at his watch. He had only half an hour if he were to catch the bus in time for his train home from Inverness. He started methodically on the documents, casting his eye swiftly through everything to see if it provided any worthwhile information.

He had been sifting his way through the paper for fifteen minutes when he came across a long, brown envelope bearing the name of solicitors in Inverness. He drew out the document and opened it. 'WILL OF LUKE SMIDDY.' It was dated the previous year. Mr Chrimes felt excitement creeping over him as he started to read. 'I LUKE SMIDDY of Roseacre House, Inverneilen, in the county of Inverness-shire hereby revoke all former wills and testamentary dispositions made by me and declare this to be my last will...'

The church clock struck the three-quarter hour and Mr Chrimes confirmed the time with his watch before working his way down to the important part of the document.

Luke had left £1,000 to the secretary of his company, £1,000 to a Miss Sheila

O'Donovan, £10,000 to Terence James Gil-michael, and … Mr Chrimes read the next two lines three times to make sure he had not made a mistake … 'my cricket bat, last used for Old Skelhamians against Skelham Grammar School, to my nephew, Matthew Luke…'

'Well, I'll go the foot of our stairs,' exclaimed Mr Chrimes.

He read through the bequests once again. Just those four, and the only thing he was giving to his one surviving blood relative, was a cricket bat. The remainder went to cancer research. Mr Chrimes looked at the nephew's full name again. Of course, the initials! Now it all fell into place. He must warn … the sound of a car crunching along the drive made him remember his position – that of a trespasser. A criminal. He folded the will and pushed it back into its envelope. His hands had started to shake and he had to take extreme care not to release the desk lid as he lifted it. He closed the lid and clumsily turned the key before replacing it in the bottom drawer. The front door of the house opened, then banged shut as Mr Chrimes slid out of the chair and moved swiftly and stealthily to the curtains. Fortunately they reached the floor and he had just time to step behind them when he heard the door to the study opening. Then he remembered. He had not switched off the light! Mr Chrimes felt certain his heavy breathing, or the hammering of his heart, or thudding in his temple, would be heard by whoever had opened the door.

'That's funny,' came a voice which Mr Chrimes immediately recognised as belonging to James. 'I'm sure I didn't leave the light on.'

Mr Chrimes heard the sound of footsteps moving across the room, pausing to straighten the chair at the desk, then catching the leg of the table. James cursed, then muttered: 'Chilly in here. I'll close that window.'

Mr Chrimes froze behind the curtains. A thousand thoughts seemed to flash through his brain as instinct took over. James reached for the curtain and just as he was taking hold of the velvet, he was interrupted by a knock at the door. He turned immediately and switched off the light as he went through the door into the hall.

The feeling of relief flooded through Mr Chrimes's body, touching every bone and sinew and nerve end as he opened the window fully and climbed out again. He crept along the wall, and peered out at the front of the house. Luke Smiddy's Rolls Royce was standing there, and alongside it a car which he recognised immediately. It was Matt Thornton's!

Mr Chrimes decided to risk being seen, but removed his bowler and bent his head as he bustled down the drive and round the corner to safety behind the trees. His shirt was wet and clinging to his back, he noticed, when he finally relaxed on the bus to Inverness. But there was still plenty to do. He must ring Donald to warn him before he caught the train.

He had only five minutes to spare when he reached the station and he dashed towards an empty telephone box. He ran his finger down the list of codes, then took out his notebook and dialled Donald's number, Skelham 46232. As the number rang out he looked at the station clock. Only three minutes to go! 'Come on Donald, for God's sake, answer this infernal machine,' he mumbled. But there was no reply. What could he do? He had to catch this train, there wasn't another all day. Donald should be all right, thought Mr Chrimes. He'll be at that autumn fair the best part of the day. He dashed out of the box, asked a passing porter for the number of his platform, and ran through the barrier just as the guard was about to signal the train off.

Mr Chrimes flopped down in the first vacant double seat and stared out of the window. He had the answer. He could only hope Donald could last out the nine hours it would take him to get back to Skelham!

FOURTEEN

Mr Chrimes was ready to leave long before the train arrived. For the last hour of the journey he wore his bowler and gloves and gripped his attaché case firmly, ready to dash for a taxi. He rarely indulged in such luxuries, but he was in a desperate hurry to warn Donald, and get the killer into custody. He was on to the platform before the train had stopped and within seconds was sitting in the back of a taxi on the last lap of his journey. As the taxi turned the last corner, Mr Chrimes spotted Donald's car pulling away from the kerb in front of the house. He could see it wasn't Donald driving so he made a hurried mental note of its number, paid off the driver, then scampered to the front door which he hammered repeatedly with his fist. But there was no answer. There were no lights at the front of the house, so Mr Chrimes raced round to the back. There wasn't a light on anywhere in the silent house and he quickly realised that no amount of knocking was going to produce a reply. For the second time that day he looked for an open window. The meticulous Donald, however, had made certain they were all closed, and Mr Chrimes was forced to break a small window in the back door to get inside.

A swift search of the house and non-stop bellows for 'DONALD, DONALD!' produced nothing. Could Donald have been in the car he saw leaving? Not unless he was lying down! Mr Chrimes went to the telephone and got through to the police station where he was put on to Chief Inspector Harry Rackham, an old and trusted colleague. He briefly gave him the details of what he had learned that day and also the number of the car.

'I'm fairly certain 'e was driving the car, and 'e can't 'ave gone far,' declared Mr Chrimes.

'And you think he's responsible for all these deaths, Joseph, is that what you're saying?'

'As sure as my name's Joseph Chrimes, 'arry.'

'Right! I'll scc it's stopped and the driver held.'

Mr Chrimes returned to the living room, where he had deposited his attaché case on the table, and stood quietly as he looked round. The cellar! He hadn't looked in the cellar!

He ran to the cellar door and as he drew it open he heard the unmistakable sound of water as if it were slapping against the side of a boat. He switched on the light at the top of the stairs and saw, to his horror, that water was washing over the bottom few steps. He dashed back into the kitchen where he located the stop cock beneath the kitchen sink, and turned it off. He grabbed a torch from the top of the cupboard and headed back to the cellar door. As he walked, he unfastened his trousers, removing them, his shoes, socks and shirt before setting off down the cellar steps. The bottom half dozen were covered with water and by the time Mr Chrimes touched the floor of the cellar the water was up to his arm pits. The door into Donald's developing and printing room was open. Mr Chrimes shone the torch through the opening, but could see nothing but the wall and water. Slowly he edged forward, afraid of slipping and taking great care not to bump into anything. When he reached the door he leaned on the frame and shone the torch inside, sweeping it round the far wall.

Suddenly he stopped! For the second time in 12 hours, he froze as the beam of light picked out the body hanging from the metal rings. The mouth had been sealed by tape, but the terror-ridden eyes stared helplessly at the light.

Donald was a good six inches smaller than Mr Chrimes and the water was playfully licking at his chin which he was desperately holding up high like a Guardsman.

'Nothing to worry about now, Donald. Soon 'ave you out of there and back on dry land.'

The water was bitterly cold and Mr Chrimes knew if he wasn't quick he would begin to seize up. A young blood like Donald's could stand the cold longer, but when you're getting old…

Cautiously, Mr Chrimes forced himself across to Donald. He held his arms high out of the water and kept the beam of the torch shining on the pitiful object facing him. As he got nearer, he could see that Donald had been tied by the wrists to the iron rings in the wall. He tore off the tape in his mouth, then set about unfastening the rope. The rings were just above the level of the water, and with the torch in one hand, Mr Chrimes had only one free hand with which to claw at the knots. In desperation he used his teeth as well and it was fully five minutes before the first hand was freed. Donald, meanwhile, had been gasping and sobbing. 'Thank God! Thank God you've come. I'd given up hope! I didn't think I'd a chance, then when I heard you moving about and you didn't come down. Oh God, I thought, don't let him go, don't let him go. Dear God, dear God...'

'There you are, Donald,' panted Mr Chrimes as he freed the hand. 'Can you manage the other while I turn the tap off and pull out the plug?' He laughed hurriedly and nervously and set off towards where the sink was located. 'Over 'ere, isn't it?'

'Yes, against the wall.'

Mr Chrimes found the sink by walking into it, and quickly felt for the plug. He pulled it out, and after turning off the tap, he pushed his fast-freezing body back towards Donald.

''Ere, you 'old the torch. I'll do that knot.'

'There's my feet as well,' said Donald. 'He tied them together. That's only tape though. He just wrapped it round and round. It should come off easily enough.'

Mr Chrimes soon had the other hand free, but Donald declined to tackle his feet.

'Then you'll just 'ave to wait till the water

goes down.'

'Oh no,' cried Donald. 'I'll freeze to death.'

'Then down you go. One deep breath and you'll 'ave that tape off.'

It took three deep breaths and a lot of splashing and spluttering before Donald was able to tear away the tape. Then he took Mr Chrimes's arm and headed for the safety of the cellar steps.

Fifteen minutes later, the two men, dried and changed, with Mr Chrimes wearing a pair of Donald's underpants and a vest, sat in front of the hot fire. Donald had also enveloped himself in a huge blanket and each clutched a hot mug of tea as they went over the day's events.

'How did you know it was him?' Donald enquired.

'When I saw the will,' explained Mr Chrimes. 'As soon as I saw the name of the nephew, Matthew Luke Smiddy Bebbington, it all fell into place. Those initials! M. L. S. And the first name, Donald. You said Malcolm, didn't you?'

'I thought it was, Mr Chrimes. It had been a long time.'

'You see, that's 'oo Luke meant when 'e told me to ask Matt. Said 'e knew all about it.

Luke realised then what his nephew had been doing. Anyway, I realised what 'ad 'appened as soon as I saw that. Leaving 'is only blood relative just a bat was the action of a bitter and twisted man. 'E must 'ave 'ated Bebbington a lot to cut 'im off like that.'

'He did,' confirmed Donald. 'He'd never really liked him from being a boy, but dislike turned into bitter hatred after the match.'

'Bebbington told you all this, did 'e?'

'Yes, like I told you, it was soon after we got back from the autumn fair that it all started. I sat down, in that chair, to watch television and the next thing I knew … bang. He'd hit me from behind and I was out cold. When I came to, I was fastened to the wall in the cellar. He'd gagged me and when he saw I'd come to properly, then he started the tap running. I didn't realise what he was doing at first, until the water started slopping over the side of the sink and began to creep up the wall. And all the time he was blabbering on about what Luke Smiddy had done, how he hated him, how he hated the school team. They'd been responsible for it all. He went on and on and I must admit I missed a good deal. I was thinking more about myself and how I was going to escape!'

'You say Bebbington told you Luke 'ad never liked 'im.'

'Yes. Bebbington's mother thought a lot about her brother, that's why she gave her son Luke for a second name and also gave him the family name, Smiddy. But it seems that even as a boy, Bebbington was never in his rich uncle's good books. Luke looked after his sister a bit. Nothing extravagant, but he'd help out if she was desperate, and it was him who encouraged her to move near Skelham when her husband died. It seems Luke went round to see Bebbington and his mother after the match. Ranted on about it. Talked about cheats and frauds, how dishonest they'd been, said they'd made a fool of him, and Bebbington was just as much to blame as anyone else. Bebbington protested that he'd never played for the school before, that he couldn't do anything. Luke maintained he could. If somebody had spoken up. Just one person. Just one. But no. Everybody backed off. A team decision, Luke said, and Matthew Bebbington had been a member of that team. Said he would never forgive him. Never. And from then on, the family didn't get any assistance whatsoever from Uncle Luke.'

'But why cut off 'is sister, as well. She

wasn't playing, was she?'

'It seems Luke was very cut up that day. Said if that was the way she brought up a child, to be a cheat and a fraud, he wanted no part of them. Bebbington had an idea, too, that Luke thought he was responsible for the damage to the car. That was another reason they were cut off.'

'Well, didn't you tell 'im Luke apparently knew that Joe Kenny 'ad done it?'

'I couldn't speak, could I, with all that tape in my mouth? Now and again, Mrs Bebbington would make an effort to get her brother to see sense, but he wouldn't have any of it. They'd blotted their copybooks and that was the end of them. It soured Matthew. He was quite brilliant at languages it seems, but his mother couldn't afford to send him on to university. A lot of the drive went out of him as well, and he just drifted. But he always held on to the hope that Uncle Luke would relent, that in the end it would come out all right. Bebbington knew that he and his mother were the only surviving relatives, and he felt certain that when it came to the crunch, Uncle Luke would see him right. He felt certain Luke would eventually come round. Then his mother died.'

'And Matthew Bebbington went up to Inverneilan to see Uncle Luke, didn't 'e?'

'Yes. He was the visitor Mrs McTavish was telling us about. With his mother dead, Bebbington was the only relative Luke had. And Luke was very rich. So up he went to try to smooth things out with his uncle.'

'And the answer was just the same, eh?'

'Yes. Luke told him he'd never get a penny. Not while he lived, nor when he was dead either. Told him in no uncertain terms that he could get back down to England and never bother him again.'

'It must 'ave shattered Bebbington.'

'It did. He reacted to that in very much the same way Luke Smiddy had reacted that day at the cricket match. A hatred built up inside him, growing like a canker.'

'Terrible thing, 'atred,' muttered Mr Chrimes.

'And he did just what Luke had done. Blamed the entire team for what had happened. And in the end, he decided to make every one of us pay.'

'All that terrible killing was over one mistake at a game of cricket,' mused Mr Chrimes.

'As far as Luke Smiddy and Matthew Bebbington were concerned, it wasn't a mistake, but blatant dishonesty,' said Donald.

'Yes, but just think. If that umpire 'ad 'ad 'is wits about 'im, 'e could never 'ave given 'im out. But one error, which 'e probably thought didn't matter a jot, caused all this. Do you remember 'oo it was?'

'The umpire? Bob Maitland, wasn't it? Whatever became of him?'

'I thought you'd never ask, Donald. 'E was chemistry teacher at the time, wasn't 'e? Then 'e moved down to Margate, where 'e died only recently. I learned just the other day. 'Is 'ouse went up in flames. And 'im inside it. Nobody knows 'ow it started...'

Matthew Luke Smiddy Bebbington was caught by the police ten minutes after Mr Chrimes's call to the station. The car was spotted in Gemble and after a five-mile chase towards the motorway, Bebbington was arrested. He confessed to the crimes and three months later was convicted at the Crown Court of murder, and sentenced to life imprisonment, a sentence that was followed with a strong recommendation from Mr Justice Soul that Bebbington should never be released from gaol.

Two days after the conviction, an item of news in the Daily Telegraph caught Donald's attention. He had spotted it over morning coffee, and at lunchtime he drove as fast as he dared to see Mr Chrimes. The ex-police officer was in his favourite chair in the sun lounge when Donald made his way round the side of the house.

'Have you seen this?' Donald shouted through the glass as he frantically waved his newspaper.

'Not the will, is it?' asked Mr Chrimes once Donald was inside.

'Yes, have you seen it?'

'I 'ad 'eard, Donald. Seems there was another will prepared after the one I saw. 'Arry Rackham was telling me about it on Tuesday, the day Bebbington was convicted. Seems it was drawn up not long before Luke gave up and died. What's it say, in the paper?'

'Matthew Bebbington, sentenced to life imprisonment two days ago, has been left £150,000 in the will, declared today, of his uncle, industrial magnate Luke Smiddy,' read Donald. 'One hundred and fifty thousand!' he repeated, incredulously.

Mr Chrimes chuckled. 'The old bugger did relent then, after all.'

The publishers hope that this book has given you enjoyable reading. Large Print Books are especially designed to be as easy to see and hold as possible. If you wish a complete list of our books please ask at your local library or write directly to:

Dales Large Print Books
Magna House, Long Preston,
Skipton, North Yorkshire.
BD23 4ND

This Large Print Book, for people
who cannot read normal print,
is published under the auspices of

THE ULVERSCROFT FOUNDATION